I0571561

Matters of Mortology

BY

T.M. Camp

This book is a work of fiction. All situations, events, and characters are nothing more or less than products of the author's imagination — and it's entirely possible some of you are as well. Any resemblance to persons living, dead, or somewhere in between is entirely coincidental.

Copyright © 2009 T.M. Camp
All Rights Reserved

Except for brief quotations in critical articles or reviews, no part of this book may be used, transmitted, broadcast, or otherwise reproduced in any manner or medium without receiving prior, written permission from the author. Violators will be pursued across the snowy wastes by the ravenous children of Hazard, leaving behind nothing but bones for your loved ones to mourn.
Published in the United States of America
ISBN: 978-0-9825603-0-3

Cover photo by T.M. Camp
Author photo by Kevin White

Layout and Design by Aurohn Press
www.aurohnpress.com

For my father,
who first told me the parable of the schoolyard.

And for Lucirina Telor Vevan.

"For every undertaker, there comes a day when they discover there's more to caring for the dead than the ritual preparation of cold, lifeless flesh. It is on this day — and for some, this day arrives early in their career while others must wait years before they see it — he will find all of his training, discipline, and craft are impotent. The boundary between life and death is controlled by ritual as much as a mountain range holds itself accountable to politics."

— from *A Practical Guide for Morticians (1658 Edition)*
by Charles L. Dowling

CHAPTER ONE

"In those more restrictive times, women were not permitted membership in the guild. Their singular gift — the ability to conceive, to serve as the vessel by which souls come into this world — was seen as too precious to risk. In those frontier days, when infant mortality hovered at fifty percent, life was so precious, so mortally vulnerable, that any exposure to the other side — to the dead or those who cared for them — was considered dangerous and forbidden. This was not mere superstition. It was the central pillar of the community and culture, to say nothing of our Creed."

— Philip Howard, *A Comprehensive, Contemporary History of Death*

There are few trees in my country. The low rolling hills of the region are shrouded in tall, pale grass. At night, thick mists seep into the valleys, spreading out between the high hills to smear the evening with a damp grayness.

I live outside the village in my family's ancestral home. The house sits, squat and massive, on the rise of a high hill at the end of a lonely rutted lane that bears our name. The house was built from pale gray stone that has gone dark over the years, like something from a Gothic novel. Three stories tall it stands, crowned with a broad slate roof. My grandfather's grandfather built this house the year the village was founded, the year my family received our charter from the guild.

People bring me their dead. By heritage, training, and perhaps even inclination, I am an undertaker. It is the family tradition, profession and homestead passed on from father to son down through the generations.

I mention my family but I am not married nor do I have children. At my age it is not likely that the former condition will be corrected in time to accomplish the latter.

Gazing down the short stretch of road ahead of me in this life, I hobble towards a day when this heritage and home will be abandoned, forgotten. And I despair for myself and the family I have betrayed.

Such was not always the case. Looking back, the enthusiasm I enjoyed in the early days of my service baffles me even now. With the passing of my father, I came into my own and embraced the full weight of the office with a conviction that served me well, in so much that it provided some measure of relief from the sorrow I felt over his passing — to say nothing of the pain of my own exile. So I shouldered his mantle and thereby accepted a life in service to the dead, forever separated from the living.

I had already said goodbye to my mother and sister when I began my apprenticeship five years prior, of course. But it wasn't until the formal acceptance of my commission that . . . well, suffice it to say that, with my father gone, I was truly alone for the first time in my life.

The night after I buried him, I wandered through the empty rooms of the manor — *my* manor — realizing for the first time how distant the muffled voices and footfalls sounded from the floors above. Separated by tradition and heritage, I could not (and would not ever) ascend the stairs to comfort my mother in her grief.

Death took her son and husband, both. Like my father, I do not regret this. But I sometimes dreamt of her, even long after she too was gone.

Those were more traditional and, in many ways, simpler times. The controversies that have fractured the guild beyond repair in recent years were decades away from conception when I came into my full office. As such, I started my life of service free from schism or debate and neither would distract me from matters of mortology.

Free from the chaos of the more fashionable causes of these modern times, my younger self let the natural order shape my life and service. Spring and summer brought new life into the world, while the cold months were traditionally busy ones for my caste, when Mother Death would walk in her orchards, collecting the windfall of winter. Of course, this was long before the ambitions and advances of modern medicine erected that arrogant, pharmaceutical fence to keep her out.

There was a time, early in my years of service (I will not, as so many of my contemporaries do, refer to it as my "career"), there was a time when I found myself in circumstances which forced me to question these natural rhythms, to even doubt my own faith in the boundaries of life and death itself.

I'm writing of the past, of course — just another old man wandering near the boundary of this life, looking back.

I'm writing of that time when I lost my faith.

There's a broad deck that runs across the back of my house, hanging out over the graveyard below. In my younger years, it was often my habit to sit there in the evenings and smoke a cigarette or two while my dinner was being prepared by my sister in her rooms above. I'd watch as the pale mists slowly crept in to fill the valley and surrounding countryside, parting from time to time to reveal the faint flicker of light from a neighboring homestead or the spectral outline of a headstone or monument in the graveyard below. Then the mist would slide back into place and leave me with nothing to ponder but the rolling pale tendrils twining under the faint stars above.

I have heard them say that starlight is but a memorial of a star long since faded and gone, just another monument left out for the elements to scour, obscure, and ultimately consume.

We did not think so then. In my time the stars were mysterious, yet constant and reliable.

But now science has taken even the stars from us.

One evening in those early days, I stood on the deck and filled the air with my flavored smoke — cinnamon and cloves, made special for me in the village — and felt the late winter chill creep down my throat and into my lungs, drawing tight fingers across my chest. Winter might be on the way out, but not without a fight. It had been a long season and though the snows had melted weeks earlier, harsh winter and burgeoning spring still battled over control of the soggy countryside.

Winter is Death's dominion and this past season found the two of us busier than any time I could recall to my memory. As is so often the case when my work is hectic, I found myself unable to sleep. The workload was such that I could only catch a few hours each night. Death had undone so many, and what sleep I managed to obtain was a pale, fitful imitation of true, cleansing rest.

Standing and smoking at the back of my home, I looked forward to the coming spring. The local mortality had already begun to taper off and it would soon be the midwives who found their sleep interrupted. And Death, perhaps offended by the wealth of life that spring shared with the world, she had a tendency to sulk during the warmer seasons. No doubt biding her time for the time when winter would come once more.

For my part, the spring held little for me but some renovations to the house, a few incidental maintenance projects in the graveyard. Apart from these things, I looked forward to a season of rest, of solitude.

From behind me, I heard the familiar sound of the dumbwaiter being lowered inside the house. Stubbing the cigarette out, I went back inside to where my dinner was waiting for me. As I ate, I listened to my sister's footsteps passing back and forth across the floor above as she prepared her breakfast. It had been nearly ten years since I had assumed my apprenticeship, ten years since I had last seen her face or spoken with her.

It was a hard and lonely life, but she bore it well. Although it might have been a vanity on my part, I often felt that she gave her own service to me with an honor and pride not dissimilar to my own. Not that she could easily acknowledge this pride. Since the time that I assumed our father's office, she had been forbidden to speak my name for fear of defilement or corruption. And should another speak my name aloud in her presence, she was bound by tradition to ignore the reference and acknowledge mention of only "your brother" or "your mother's son."

How times have changed.

Although she did not speak of me nor hear me spoken of — at least, not directly — and since she was forbidden to speak to me herself, the dumbwaiter in our home served as our only formal channel of communication. She left me handwritten notes which we sent back and forth when she felt it necessary to inform me of a specific piece of news or gossip that she brought home from the village.

After nearly a decade of not hearing my name — no, nor speaking it herself — I suppose that it was possible that she might have forgotten it altogether due to misuse. And, it occurs to me now, she might have even forgotten her own name as well.

Of course, I had not forgotten — although, I was permitted to speak her name only over her grave, to speak it only once she had passed the boundaries of this world and was beyond the corruption of the dead or we who serve them.

No, I had not forgotten her name. As an undertaker, no name is denied me. I shall speak them all, in the end.

My dinner finished, I set the empty dishes inside the dumbwaiter and went into my study to settle back in front of the fire with a book, as was my custom in the evenings. Above, I could hear my sister going about her nightly chores. The evening wore on and the fire burned low, filling the room with flickering shadows. I had just drifted off when a sound from the upper floors of my house drew me out of my dozing: My sister, leaving for her weekly visit to the village.

Typically speaking, and seasonal fluctuations notwithstanding, I work from dawn until dusk. My sister, on the other hand, observed an opposite schedule. All of this is, of course, to ensure that she remained protected from accidental exposure to me or my office. In their kindness, the shopkeepers and merchants of our village stayed open late to serve her.

I have heard that in these modern times, families of my caste are more inclined to set aside the old traditions and routines in favor of convenience. I do not begrudge them their lapses, for they are minor notes in the larger heresies that have risen in these later days.

How times have changed.

Even so, I do not blame them. I understand the sacrifice that such a separation imposes on everyone in a household. I understand too well that late night ache, that loneliness that deepens with the passing hours.

So often my own evenings were scored by the dull edge of insomnia, the sleepless time folding back on itself while I paced the floors and stared into the silent embers of my hearth.

Protected as she was, my sister was not safe from my restless nights. She wrote numerous notes to me on the subject, complaining that she could not stand to hear my vexed footfalls wandering through the lower floors of, she reminded me, our shared home. Despite my efforts, pharmaceutical and otherwise, to curtail these episodes, they would invariably return and I would once again wander the sleepless rooms and hallways. Fortunately, winter was nearing its end and I was hopeful that the milder season and workload would take the edge off of my insomnia as well.

But Death, I was to find out, would not be on holiday this year. My nights would prove to be far more restless and vexed than ever before.

On the cusp of that time, unknowing, I looked up from my book to see that the fire had burned low. I rose and threw an armful of dried flowers onto the embers, settling back into my chair once more. My book proved stale and soon I was dozing my way through unhappy, fretful dreams.

Hours later I woke to find the fire burned down to nothing, not even embers remained in the grate. The room was cold and a few familiar spirits flittered listlessly around the lifeless coals. I turned drowsily in my chair, falling back into sleep, tipping face first into a nightmare where I wandered barefoot through a vast field of bones. The hollow eyes stared up at me, empty and accusing.

Nightmares are commonplace in my profession. It's only natural. If there is one lesson I have learned from my many years of service, it is this: Death leaves no one untouched.

CHAPTER TWO

"The bodies of the newly dead are not debris nor remnant, nor are they entirely icon or essence. They are, rather, changelings, incubates, hatchlings of a new reality. . . . [It] is wise to treat such new things tenderly, carefully, with honor."

— Thomas Lynch, *The Undertaking: Life Studies from the Dismal Trade*

I have always awakened with the sun. I am never able to sleep past dawn. Nor is it my custom to eat breakfast. Instead, I rise and dress quickly so that I might have more time to savor my morning stroll down the hill to the graveyard below. Over the years, I and my predecessors have worn a bare path through the tall grass — each son tracing daily over his father's steps, performing the same tasks, fulfilling the same responsibilities, serving the same God. Few mornings go by, even now, when I walk that path without thinking of my own father.

In the last years of his service, just prior to his death, my father spoke more and more often of our craft. Not of the usual points of instruction, the minutia of our labors — no, instead he spoke more and more of the grand scope of our efforts, the spiritual, metaphysical, and cultural resonance of our work. He became a philosopher, a visionary, perhaps even a mystic. Even then, before the faintest hint of what was to come, even then he anticipated the coming schism, the fierce machines of debate that tore our guild apart in recent years. He saw and predicted it all. Like the magician in the parable, he grieved over the future.

He was very wise. I miss him every day. I miss him still.

"A study was conducted," he told me one afternoon during our last year together, while we worked to prepare a client for burial. "A study of children in a schoolyard — how they played together, how they behaved when their teachers were watching and when they were not. There was a large fence that ran around the perimeter of the schoolyard and the children ran and played freely throughout, exploring and enjoying their world right up to the boundary. From time to time, one of the children would venture to climb over the fence — either out of rebellion or following their own sense of adventure. The child would be corrected accordingly and play would continue on as before.

"After a few months, the children arrived at school one day to find that their fence had been removed."

My father paused to wipe the sweat from his eyes. We'd been deeply engrossed in the rites of Preparation — perhaps the most difficult phase of an undertaker's work, given the physical and emotional effort needed to work with cold, lifeless flesh. Mopping his brow, he gestured for me to hand him the long, thin "taming" knife so rarely used today and continued his work and story.

"Once the fence was gone, the children no longer played as before. Instead of roaming freely, they huddled together in small groups clustered at the center of the playground far away from the undefined, unknown boundary. After observing and interviewing the children, the researchers concluded that, with the fence gone, the playground had become a place of uncertainty. The children were afraid to stray too far, lest they inadvertently cross the unseen boundary."

"So they huddled together, whispering and afraid even to play where they knew it must be safe."

He handed the knife back to me and I wiped it carefully on my apron in the over-and-under ritual gesture I had learned at the Academy.

He nodded approvingly. "This is what happens when boundaries are removed — freedom is stifled and we become slaves to fear."

And with that, he made the sign of the great god Terminus and gestured for me to hand him a spool of wire.

I miss him still.

And, writing these words, I find the true start to my story — not with a dry catalogue of my office or family heritage, nor in the self-pitying superiority of an old man waving tradition at his younger colleagues.

No, my story begins in the graveyard, winter still lingering on as I walked down the hill with memories of my father haunting me as the rising sun bruised the sky. As I recall, there was a cold wind that rasped through the high grass, as chill and unpleasant as my memories are to me now.

At the halfway point between the house and the graveyard where the slope of the hill finally levels out, there stands the masonshack. Early in my time of service — in the time that I write of — the Mason was the only companion in an otherwise truly solitary occupation. In addition to attending to the physical upkeep of the yard itself, the mason's main labor is spent providing headstones and monuments for the dead.

My own Mason was a good fellow. Decent, hardworking despite his years — he had come to our family in my father's first year of service, long before my sister and I were born. Now, he had perhaps only a few years of service left in him before retirement. Masons, unlike my caste, do not work until they pass beyond the boundary of this life. Rather, they remain in service until their health or age dictates otherwise. The nature of their labor and exposure to the elements make them sometimes subject to painful arthritic tremors, rendering their tools unwieldy in their hands. And it is thus, more often than not, that their craft is lost.

Our Mason was not yet at the point, but it was apparent to me that retirement was imminent. I knew he could feel its cold grasp on him, chiseling away more of his strength with each passing day.

It was my custom in the mornings to rap on his door as I passed the small stone masonshack, continuing on down to the graveyard. Once he'd risen and donned the coveralls and scarf he wore in any weather, rain or shine, Mason would trundle along after with his wheelbarrow down the path, bringing the various tools we might need for the day's labor.

That long ago morning however, while I was yet halfway down the hill, I was surprised to see that he was outside, slumped on the little stone stoop outside the shack's door — head hung low, his arms cradling something close to his chest. Even from a distance, his sobs reached me.

He'd found her in the graveyard long before dawn, when he was making his final rounds before turning in. At first glance, he'd thought her a memorial banner forgotten after one of the recent funerals, an old garland gone dry and brown. But as he drew closer, his old eyes filled with recognition and tears at the sight of the dog sprawled limply across a gravestone, casually flung there — her neck broken, rudely gutted from throat to haunches.

He said her name once, there in the shallow night. And then he took her in his arms and headed home, where I was to find him a few hours later . . . sitting there, stroking her fur gently, whispering to her some secret sorrow that my ear strained to hear.

His eyes met mine as I approached. "It's a cruel thing to lose her this way, I can tell you, sir."

His voice shook and he looked away.

Murmuring my sympathies, I released him from his service for the day and continued on towards the graveyard in a much more sober frame of mind. I picked through the plots, gathering up any flowers that had begun to wither. Nothing will distress a mourner more than to find dead flowers on the grave that they came to visit.

It was rare for me to work alone. Usually the morning chores were punctuated with Mason's chatter. Although I was used to tuning him out as I worked, the early silence unsettled me. I kept seeing his eyes, those old eyes clouded with rheum and sadness. I had often thought his life of solitude — a somewhat more compact analogue of my own — disagreed with him, ran contrary to his nature and temperament. He seemed to revel in conversation and companionship, almost starving for it in a desperate sort of way.

My father once told me that a few years after Mason's arrival, he petitioned for permission to obtain a dog — ostensibly to serve as evening sentry in the graveyard. My father, reading the deep loneliness in the man's eyes, offered his agreement and approval. And, apparently, it did the trick. Mason's vigor improved with the arrival of the animal and his days and nights were brighter for the company. He called her his Lady and she trotted behind him faithfully as he performed his duties, ever attentive to his rambling, one-sided conversations.

And now she is gone, I thought to myself as I filled my arms with dead flowers. The poor creature had been unfortunate prey to some winter-starved animal or other. While it's rare for beasts to find their way into my graveyard, it is not unknown. During the first year that my father took up his office, the yard was beset by a vast parliament of rooks that lingered for three days and nights. They swarmed over the graves, perching on the headstones, shattering their air with their vulgar cries until one morning they were gone as though they had never been. No sign remained of them, save for the vague artistry of the guano-spattered monuments. In their absence, my father told me, the silence was uncomfortable, disturbing.

And we've even seen the occasional wolf, that outcast child of Hazard, prowling about in lean times. After a few days, they move on in search of bones not so dry and not so old as ours.

No doubt Lady had met her savage end at the teeth of such a beast.

Lost in thought, it took me some time to realize that I had gathered a huge pile of dried flowers — far more than usual. On an ordinary day, I might collect an armful or two as fuel for my fireplace. Yet on that day, I found dead flowers waiting for me at nearly every grave. All of the flowers and wreaths had withered, as though dried out in the summer sun. Only a few graves here and there — those decorated with the white moly — remained untouched by the blight.

As I set another armful on top of the knee-high heap of flowers, I heard Mason shuffling up behind me. His cap was off and his eyes darted from my feet to my face, then back again, his features overcome with a mixture of shame and sadness.

I told him that he needn't bother with work today if he didn't feel up to it.

He begged my pardon. "I don't particularly feel like anything but working today, really."

He shuffled his feet and dug one hand into a pocket, producing three small coins. Before I could protest, he thrust the money at me.

"Sir, I would like, if at all possible, to buy your service today. It would do my Lady a great honor if you gave her your attentions. She was too good a friend to me to just let her rot in a hole where what had done her in might come back and dig her up again."

I was overcome and, misreading my silence, Mason dropped his head.

"I apologize, sir. I didn't mean the insult. I know she's just a dog and dog's is for holes. Forgive my presuming too much."

He shook his head and turned to shuffle off. "I think I might take today for myself, after all, since you offered."

I caught his arm, calling him a dear fellow and saying I would be honored to attend to his Lady.

He blinked at me, eyes awash with grateful tears. "It's not beneath you, sir?"

I assured him it would be beneath me to turn my back on such a faithful servant.

He dug in his pocket once more but I waved him off, the payment unnecessary. He grunted, reluctant to give up, insistent that I take payment. "It'll make things proper, sir. For her."

Finding that I could not refuse him without insulting him, I accepted his coins. God only knew how long he'd been saving them. More likely than not they'd been set aside to pay for his own burial.

The transaction reluctantly completed, he and I went back into his shack to gather the equipment we would need. The pile of dried flowers remained forgotten back in the graveyard.

Chapter Three

"An entire mythology has grown up around the process of dying. Like most mythologies, it is based on the inborn psychological need that all human kind shares. The mythologies of death are meant to combat fear on the one hand and its opposite — wishes — on the other."

— Sherwin B. Nuland, *How We Die*

The masonshack was made up of a single room dominated by the large slab-topped table at the center, upon which the dead are laid. On the walls, tools of Preparation are hung within easy reach: Aprons, blades, saws, wires, scoops, and the like. In cupboards below the table are stored the various fluids and wrappings of Preservation — some prophylactic, some treated with fragrant and exotic spices. In those same cupboards you will find the tools of Restoration: Cosmetics, sutures, and even limited prosthetics. It is rare when Mother Death leaves her children in a state comely to the eyes of mourners.

At the start and finish of each Preparation, I wash my hands in the cast iron sink — a marriage of symbolism and utility that my contemporary colleagues fail to value or observe.

The only light in the room comes from a small skylight set into the roof above. This prevents us from allowing our work to stretch into the evening, regardless of how busy the season. Day or night, no light ever burns in the masonshack for fear of attracting corpse candles like moths. These are mischievous and many an apprentice working late by candlelight has been spooked by their pranks. This practice remains one of the few old superstitions from my generation which lingers on in modern times, though I suspect that the evening limit to the workday has more to do now with a younger generation's desire to socialize (so scandalous in my time) rather than sincere spiritual considerations.

After all, the shack is the Mason's workplace as well as his dwelling — the sink his bath, the slab his pallet. His is a meager life, shared with the dead.

Once the rites of Preparation and Restoration are complete, the casket is introduced to serve as the container of the corpse in this world as well as the soul's transport across the boundary to the next. Once again, an integration of symbol and utility, both in this world and the one beyond.

Traditionally, the coffin is provided by the family and filled with mementos of the deceased. Outside of our caste, it is a common misconception that my kind appropriate these cherished items as gratuities due our office. While I cannot speak for my brothers in the dismal trade, I can only assure you that my father trained me to treat these mementos as sacred objects, holy and untouchable. As their owner passes, so, too, they go with him.

Graveside, the following collect is offered in conjunction with the rites of Commitment:

> *Depart, O soul, out of this world*
> *In the name of God, Terminus,*
> *who drew the boundaries*
> *of your life and death.*
> *In the name of God, Terminus,*
> *who gathers you to Himself.*
> *In the name of God, Terminus,*
> *who holds out His gentle hand*
> *to guide your passage.*
> *May your rest be found in peace,*
> *and your dwelling within the walls of joy.*

As the casket is lowered, the gathered mourners offer this prayer:

Into your all-encompassing arms,
O God, we commend your servant.
Guide them, O Lord, across this
boundary and through the shadow,
hold back the unseen dread
with your mighty hand
and grant this one safe passage.
As you walk the boundaries, Lord,
do not forget we who wait within.

In all things,
around all things,
and beyond all things.
Amen.

It is at this point in the rites when testimonies familial and familiar are offered. Special messages or farewells from female relatives are delivered by the eldest male relative present. As it is said: "We do not mourn; we remember."

In those times, women could not even observe the period of Remembrance for those who had passed. I do not say these things to show my approval of them. I realize that the world has moved on. And yet, as a product of my time and the inheritor of the traditions of that previous generation, I accepted — and still accept — all freedom offered within those boundaries, and all restraint as well. But, yes, the world has moved on.

Women, I am told, may speak for the dead now.

Once the testimonies are offered and the time of Remembrance has begun, the grave is sealed and the marker is placed upon it.

Of course, if a family or deceased is not of the Faith, they may specify their own rites for Preparation and Committal — although I will not perform these as I am not permitted to homage or importune a false god. In such cases, these pagan ceremonies are performed by a suitable alternative — either a priest or observant family member.

In the box so carefully crafted by her loving master, Lady was surrounded by meager trappings from her life: A tin bowl, the wool blanket, a wire brush. Each of these Mason touched briefly under her nose before laying the object beside her. Then we bore her down to the yard and laid her to rest in the grave he had prepared.

He stood there, cap in hand, as I pronounced the rites. Once the ceremony was finished, I completed my rounds in the graveyard, leaving him to offer her any private testimonials he could manage through his sobs.

Feeling the flush of shame and guilt for it, I wondered how I would get through my day with the cloud of his sorrow hanging over me. I needn't have worried. There were other distractions waiting for me that day.

CHAPTER FOUR

"By foreign hands thy dying eyes were closed,
By foreign hands thy decent limbs composed,
By foreign hands thy humble grave adorned,
By strangers honoured, and by strangers mourned!"

— Alexander Pope, from *A Prologue for Addison's Cato*

The grave gaped wide beneath me, a spray of dried flowers hanging limply from my hand. Flat, dull rage filled me at the sight of such desecration.

He had been so young when they brought him to me — one of those rare times when Death leaves behind a trace of life's bloom to mock those who mourn.

They were foreigners, his family, from the Far East and only recently settled in this land. A few seasons prior they had entombed themselves in a large manor on the outskirts of the village, living nearly as remote as myself. They rarely visited town or sought the company of others. Yet when the boy passed, they brought him to me.

"He had bad blood," the boy's uncle shook his head, the aged skin of his neck wrinkling like silk. The boy's mother, past her childbearing years and therefore immune to defilement, stood behind him — little more than a smudge of face behind her veil.

I could see the glitter of her eyes through the thick lace and nothing more. And yet, even those thrilled me, unaccustomed as I was to contact with women. I am ashamed to say that reminding myself of my office and heritage did little to balance out the erratic churning of my blood under that gaze.

And her voice...

They spoke to each other softly, like birds — cooing words passed from mouth to ear, gentle voices speaking a language I would never know. And yet I still hear it sometimes, as I drift off into sleep in my lonely manor.

Her voice...

A stoic people, they brought forth no tears.

The boy's uncle was a priest of their faith. As their rites and practices were foreign to me, I agreed that he should perform the service.

Forgoing the usual rites, they brought the child in a carved cedar coffin so fragrant that it nearly overshadowed the lush incense the uncle lit at the outset of his ceremony. I do not know where they found such a rarity, that wood. It was certainly not from our region.

Intrigued by the priest's atonal chanting, I watched as he enclosed the boy's coffin — the wood dark as old blood — and committed him into the hands of unfamiliar gods.

Once the final stick of sandalwood had been burnt and the last wave of gnarled fingers shaped a final mystic sigil in the air above the coffin, the uncle stepped back.

Mason then came forward to close the grave, sucking his teeth in suspicious disapproval. His clumsy spade rudely punctuated the elegance of the ceremony.

I watched as the two of them walked away through the graveyard, mother and uncle, each supporting the other. I strained to hear their faint murmurs until the uncomprehending mists swallowed them.

"Not proper," Mason said, wiping the grime of his hands on the seat of his pants, "With their strange, smelly gods and their odd ways."

I did not answer. For all of my tradition, I believe that even strangers deserve the respect of my caste when Death comes. None have ever been turned away from my yard. I know that it is more in vogue now to adopt stricter, almost partisan attitudes towards faith; so strange when liberalism reigns over most other issues. And so they create partitions among them, keeping people in their place — even the dead.

I did not do so then and I still would not do so now. Such prejudice of office would bring shame upon my family name. For what do any of us deserve but a proper death?

"Bad blood," I said to myself, gazing down on that torn and desecrated grave and feeling the violation to my core. I climbed down to inspect the coffin and assure myself that it was still intact. Whether prank, vandalism, or even theft . . . this desecration was an immense insult to me and my office, to say nothing of the sheer, outright rudeness towards the dead. The great God, Terminus who set his seal on such places, did not abide such trespass.

I returned with regret, rousing Mason from his sorrow so that he might refill the boy's grave.

Despite his prejudice, he was profoundly shocked at the vandalism and I could see he took it to heart.

"This," he said to me, "This is something that is not done. Plain and simple, people don't do this."

I could do nothing but agree and leave him to his work.

CHAPTER FIVE

"Vandalism is a natural by-product of the living and the dead coexisting in such close cohabitation. There are those who believe that the dead return to haunt their former homes long after they have passed on, regardless of whether or not the current residents have extended an invitation. It should come as no surprise then when the living sometimes intrude into the domain of the dead. If they can haunt us with impunity, so then might we do the same of them."

— Stephen Hubble, *A Practical Guide for the Death Trade Entrepreneur*

The light in my library falls across my desktop in fragments, a shattered rainbow cast from the stained glass window above. On bright days, the room is filled with gorgeous strokes of light casting broad swaths of color across the book-lined walls of my study.

My collection is extensive, populated by not only my own books but by all of those handed down through the preceding generations. It is an obvious metaphor, I know, but I have often thought that each book stands on its shelf much like the stones in the graveyard below, marking the place where a lifetime has been stored away.

The similarity even extends further, for with the stones they also share a cool perfume of dust and well-tended age. And each book, like each stone, holds a singular personality that I treasure as much as any flesh and blood companion.

Even now, the titles and authors glint dully at me from the shadows — smiling, winking, enticing. As my life is a solitary one, my books are the only friendly population that my occupation will allow.

This room lies at the center of my house. It is the foundation, the support, and it is the heart of me.

It is where I spend my time.

And so it is where I went to mull things over after I returned home, after I found the vandalism in the graveyard.

As a child, I spent much of my time poring over my father's books. His tastes were not so broad as my own, limited chiefly to professional journals and technical manuals. Dry though they were, these fascinated me. Yet my earliest memories were not of these, but rather of the broken light cast by that high window. Many an afternoon I spent running my fingers through the scattered puzzle — maddeningly insubstantial, impossible to restore.

Even that familiar, shattered light would not soothe me that day. The desecration of the grave had been immense — the marker tilted askew and the grave torn open as if by animals. But no animal leaves muddy handprints behind. No beast wears boots. Whoever had done this, I decided, had come from the village with the purpose in mind. This was no youthful prank. Nothing like this had ever happened before — no, nor since, either.

Someone came to do this thing, someone from within the boundaries of my community, someone who would — in all likelihood — one day be buried here in my yard. It was unbearable to think on it.

They had come, I knew as certain as anything, because the boy was a foreigner.

I thought of contacting the authorities, but our scheduled session on the circuit was still four weeks off and I had no faith in the deductive abilities of the addled postmaster who doubled as our local, itinerant deputy.

And there was the family to consider. As their traditions were unfamiliar to me, I fretted that perhaps such a situation required special rites to purify what had been desecrated. To inform them of the event, however, was also to admit some lack on my part. Mason was right, after all, it never should have occurred. And yet, it had.

The choice was clear to me. It is my obligation to serve the living as well as the dead. Despite reputation, despite pride — in fact, because of these things — the boy's family must be told.

Though they had not requested or required my ministrations or comfort in their grief, they might at least accept my apologies. They must be told, if for nothing else then for the sake of that boy they buried.

My decision made, I set out to deal with this unpleasant errand immediately. I knew I would not sleep well with it camped on the periphery of my conscious mind all night long. So, taking up my stick and shrugging on a heavy coat, I set out walking.

The road was rough and scarred from the long winter, the harsh rain and snow. Deep ruts crossed here and there — the tracks of the cartwheels tracing through the network of roads, connecting each house to the village and with each other. The trails leading to and from my manor were broader, more shallow than the rest. Most animals shun my presence on instinct. Horses will scream and stamp at the sight, even the scent, of me and my kind. And so the dead are brought to me on wagons with iron wheels, pulled by men.

I do not know why the wheels are iron. This was not taught in my schooling. It is a tradition older than my or my father's knowledge. And I have never read of it in my studies.

The bitter wind slapped my face as I walked, chapping my lips and drawing them dry. All around, the tall grasses hissed in the wind like the thin tails of a thousand frightened cats protesting my passage.

"Even nature recognizes Death's servant," or so the proverb goes.

Now, in the recounting of this story, I admit there is a temptation to gift myself with a greater awareness of the situation than that which I possessed at the time. Honesty dictates I confess that I did not recognize the true nature of what I was facing, not until it was too late.

God meant for me to struggle with far worse matters than butchered dogs and desecrated graves. In the end, my struggle would drift across the boundary between the physical and the spiritual. And not all of we who fought made it back across once more.

On my way to inform the boy's family of what had occurred, I thought on Mason's Lady and the graveyard vandalism. And, despite this old man's vanity, I must admit that I did not link the two events in my mind.

After a time and a distance on the frozen roads, I came to the gate of the house I sought, so stark against the overcast sky. There was a small bundle of fruit hanging from the crossbar of the gate, a mourning custom from their country perhaps. I entered, noting that all of the fruit had been pecked at by birds.

Within, their house was surrounded by a second wall of stacked stone, somewhat lower than the outer barrier. I passed along up the lane and went through a second gate, also hung with dried fruit, drained to a husk.

On the other side, I found myself face to face with a demon.

The creature was drawn back as though startled by my appearance, raising one paw in savage shock, body tense and ready to spring. Unthinking, I lashed out with my walking stick, barking a short grunt of surprise and fear.

My blow bounced off the statue — for, of course, that is what it was — and immediately I cast an eye up to the windows of the house, praying that no one had observed my foolishness.

After taking a moment to regain our composure, the stone demon and I regarded each other in a more respectful light.

And then I continued on up the walkway, passing through a magnificent garden stunning in its sublimity. Obvious care had been taken with the design, and the order was admirable. Small paths ran off into secluded clearings. Patterned stones chattered quietly in a shallow creek bed. Brassy shadowfish swept along the bottom of rock-lined pools. It was a place of gentle reflection and calm, so much so that I might have dallied a bit in my walk to the front door of the house. I do not often have the opportunity to experience quiet and peace without the presence of Death there also, let alone such an elegant environment.

And I must admit that I felt no small measure of guilt for bringing more painful news to this household, to see the sorrow redoubled in those veiled eyes and to be the cause of it. I wondered, gazing down into a small pool where fleet shadows swam, how long a woman was obliged to wear the veil of mourning in their tradition?

I wondered over the color of her eyes — a momentary indulgence that I regret, even now.

Reminding myself that she had lost her son, that she was most likely twice my age and as inaccessible to me as her native land, I turned towards the house.

Although an iron bell hung to one side of the door, I knocked. In those times any musical instrument, even bells, were forbidden to my caste as it was once believed that their tones summoned whatever spirits might be nearby. Current learned thought has, through controlled experiment, conclusively determined that such is not the case. And so modernity liberates us all from the confinement of another antique superstition, even me — though I still do not care for the sound of bells, not even now.

After a few moments, the door was opened by the boy's uncle. He nodded in greeting and, before I could offer a word of explanation, gestured me to enter. Closing the door behind me, the uncle led me through a hallway to an elegant parlor draped in embroidered rugs and tapestries.

We sat opposite each other in matching velvet chairs. The boy's uncle regarded me with patient respect and, taking my cue, I began to speak.

I was brief, having long before learned that bad news is best delivered quickly and without adornment. Once I'd finished describing the vandalism of his nephew's grave, I offered my apologies.

For a time, the uncle remained silent — his eyes closed, long fingers twirling the tendrils of his thin beard.

I waited as patiently as I could, casting a glance around the room overpopulated with ivory, jade, and porcelain figurines. It was a bit too much for my Spartan sensibilities. I tried to imagine what it would be like to live in a place so cluttered, to wake up every morning surrounded by fragile beauty. I wondered if the privilege of gazing into those dark eyes unveiled was worth giving up a life of clean, pure order.

I fixed my gaze on a small lacquered bowl sitting beneath the uncle's chair. It appeared to hold half a dozen or so common hen's eggs. Shifting in my seat, my heels nudged something at my feet — something soft that hissed and flickered forward across the rug to leap up into the uncle's lap.

Baleful eyes glared back across the room at me.

The uncle chuckled. "I am sorry for the rudeness of little Jīngqí," he said, his hands stroking the sleek bundle nestled in his lap. "He has never learned his manners, and I fear I indulge him far beyond what is good for him."

The creature raised its head and volleyed shrill little curses at me for a moment.

I lowered my feet back to the floor, thankful that I had not compounded my shame by jumping up on the chair.

"These things you tell me of," the uncle continued, his eyes closing once more, "While they distress me, they do not concern me. As I see it, your duty was tested and found remiss. And so, the damage must now by your duty be mended."

I agreed, stinging a little at his honesty. I assured him that I was more than willing to do whatever he instructed me.

He drew breath into his lungs with the care of one who knows the limits of their life too well, his eyes still closed.

I had the impression that I might have interrupted him. I resolved to be more courteous, reminding myself that even the rhetorical shapes with which these people built their conversations might be very different from my own.

After a careful moment he continued, remarking that it was good I was so willing to oblige their wishes. "In our country," he told me, "When such a thing occurs, it is the custom to leave the grave open and exposed so that any evil or impurity which might have been trapped within can escape once more."

"Open and exposed?" I could not help but ask the question, incredulous.

The bright-eyed animal chittered, scolding me for my outburst. It slithered off of its master's lap and scampered beneath the chair.

The boy's uncle opened his eyes, gazing at me patiently.

"It is our custom and our wish," he said firmly.

I did not want to argue, but I was confused by the remedy he had prescribed. "Surely leaving the grave open would only serve to contaminate it further?"

After a long, disapproving moment, he said "I assure you of our custom — something of which you admit to know little, if anything."

I nodded at the curt tone in his voice.

"In these situations, the grave must be left open. That is the wish of the family. Your function is to fulfill that wish, is it not?"

I agreed that this was the case.

"Then please do so, and without hesitation. Reopen the grave, expose the casket for an evening so that whatever corruption might be resting there can finally be released."

He sighed for a moment, closing his eyes. "And then, at dawn, seal the casket tightly and refill the grave so that the desecration cannot return."

He opened his eyes, staring directly into my own. "Those are the wishes of the family. This is the custom of our land."

He was interrupted by a sharp sound from beneath his seat. I lowered my gaze to see the little weasel-like creature skulking there with an egg clutched between its paws, chipping away at the shell, sucking it dry.

The uncle rose and I followed suit, the small feral eyes below his chair following me as he led me from the room.

At the front door, he stopped with his hand on the knob. "Please. I believe the ninth regret approaches. Only you can prevent this."

And then he ushered me out and closed the door, leaving me to wonder what it was he had meant by that odd turn of phrase. Chalking it up to the capriciousness of language, I left down the path through the gardens, patting the stone demon as I passed.

The dried fruit rattled on the gate behind me as I headed for home.

Chapter Six

"That is the cuckoo, you say. I cannot hear it."

— Edward Thomas, *The Cuckoo*

I awoke late in the night, a sound uprooting me out of a deep slumber. I sat up with a start. The book that had been resting on my chest tumbled to the floor.

I'd been dreaming, something heavy pressing on me, weighing me down. Ancient eyes held mine fixed, immobilized . . . and then it let out a hideous, piercing scream.

I cast about for a moment there in the shadows, my mind a jumble of dream memories and glimpses of reality around me. The room was dim, the fire had burned down and the air hung low with the heady fragrance of smoldering flowers. I repositioned myself on the couch and was just starting to wander back down that dark road into sleep once more when a long piercing cry rang out in the night.

Upright, half standing, I waited quivering in the dim light, resonating with the echo of that cry. My familiars cowered in the corners of the library, rolling their milky eyes at me, mouths agape. Their misty frames shuddered as each new cry rang out.

Outside, a bird called out from somewhere off in the fields surrounding the manor — a thin, wavering sound, full of wandering and loneliness. It was not a call I had heard before but, as I have written already, strange migrations are not unheard of in this region.

The cry was repeated several times in the space of a few minutes. My thoughts turned to Mason, alone in his shack. I imagined him staring at the thin door that provided the only security for his modest home, listening to the strange cries echo around him.

I went to the window and looked out into the night, but there was little I could see through the thick shroud of mist that settled over the graveyard. Then, a faint flicker caught my eye — a brief moment when the strands of mist and shadow parted long enough to let it escape.

Mason. Of course, he would not let fear bottle him. He would rise and, taking up one of the heavier implements he used for his work, he'd venture out into the night to investigate.

I imagined him there, stalking through the graveyard with the upraised lantern in his hand as he tracked the foreign cries to their lonely source. Perhaps he would think that they came from the creature that had so savagely dispatched his pet. But no bird I knew of could capably commit such cruel violence. Whatever the source of that lonely sound, however strange, it could not be the culprit.

But that would not stop Mason from investigating. He too had felt the pang of guilt for not preventing the previous night's vandalism. Even unfamiliar bird calls would rouse his renewed diligence. He had his pride, after all.

Mason...

How he'd glared and sucked his teeth when I delivered the instructions that afternoon from the boy's uncle. He did not approve of the directives we were to follow in dealing with the desecrated grave.

"It's not a proper thing," he said to me. "Why go digging that child up again? He's restful now, amn't he?"

Neither slothful nor quarrelsome by nature, he must have felt strongly to offer such resistance to these instructions. Though, I'm sure, he also didn't relish the idea of reopening the grave once again. All told, his shovel would have to turn over that dirt five times by the time all was completed.

I shrugged, gazing upward. The sky was growing dark with the coming of evening and there was work left for both of us to accomplish before nightfall.

"It is their wish," I told him as simply as I could. "It is their right."

He turned away with a nod, uncharacteristically sulky, and I left him to his work.

He was still working when I retired — well, retreated really — to my fire and my books. I might have stayed on to help him, I know. But I was tired, and tired of the fretful thoughts that had run through my mind all day, like a pack of wolves taking down a deer in winter.

No matter. In the morning it would be finished and we could fill up the grave and go on with our work as before.

The cry was repeated throughout the night. Sometimes it came from far off, plaintive and faint. So close at other times that it sounded as though the bird was roosting beneath my window. Whether it was a single bird wandering alone or a flock calling to each other, I could not tell.

The calls were, at times, uncannily articulate — nearly human, even. The utterances so alien to my ears, I passed this off as merely a fancy born of an unpleasant dream.

All through the night the mournful calls went on, pealing out their lonesome dirge while I sat awake listening, my mind unable to fashion the shape that might contain such a cry.

Eventually, I fell back into a troubled sleep. From time to time a particularly close cry would jerk me once again out of my shallow nightmares before fading off into the fields once more, leaving me to drift back into shadow and slumber.

My dreams that night swarmed with dark-bodied wasps gliding through the shadows between the stars.

On and on this went, throughout the night, the dreadful calls tapering off when the first grey streaks of dawn were visible in the east. Only then, with a final, wrenching anguish, did the calls melt away.

Shaky and weak from lack of sleep, it was not until I heard my sister's footfalls in the room above that I thought of her safety.

The immediate guilt of that selfish omission weighed heavily on me.

As I said before, night was her waking time and surely the cries must have frightened her as well. I felt ashamed that all of my thoughts had been only of myself — fleetingly of Mason — but forgotten her completely.

I listened to her steps, as I so often had in the past, trying to translate their rhythm into words. A code of footfalls and paces which, if deciphered correctly, would disclose to me her very thoughts. But the sounds fell hollow, revealing nothing at all.

Finally, the dawn long past, I rose and prepared myself for the day ahead. As I dressed, I heard the sound of the dumbwaiter being lowered from above. Inside, I found a sheet of gray paper, folded twice upon itself, containing within a single line of my sister's delicate script:

Did you hear the birds last night?

I smiled, sharing the moment with her. Although we are twins, we do not share a special link of spirit or mind as I have heard some do.

It was not the first time I regretted the strictures of my caste which prevented us from sharing any true communion. We subsisted on such meagre fare, these dry wafers. Yet her words seemed alive to me. I felt the thrill in them, in the slant of her letters, in the haste with which the nib had scored the page.

The morning was chill and dank. The night had left me out of sorts and in need of some distraction. As was my custom — and as had been my father's custom — I typically went in to town once a week for supplies. While there, I took time for a few personal errands to collect my special made cigarettes and to pay a visit to a local bookshop so that I might pick over whatever selections Burke — the garrulous proprietor — had set aside for me.

Usually on that day, I would work in the graveyard until noon, saving my trip for later in the day. It was an incentive to finish my labor quickly, a little trick I had picked up from my father.

But that morning, I turned my feet towards the village. It occurred to me as I passed out of the lane beyond the manor that I ought to check in with Mason first and see how things had fared during the night.

But the lure of Burke's shop was too great and my desire for conversation — even for Burke's clever, albeit maddening conversation — was too strong to resist. Nor should I have any need to. I'd worked hard and the season was coming to an end. My service would not atrophy if I set it aside for the afternoon.

Looking back, I cannot quite see how it would have mattered if I had gone down to the graveyard that morning instead of breaking my custom. What had happened could not be undone. And a few hours would matter to no one.

So on I went through the mist and fog, heading for town and ignorant of what the night had left waiting for me in the graveyard.

What had happened could not be undone.

CHAPTER SEVEN

"Hoc patrium est, potius consuefacere filium
Sua sponte recte facere, quam alieno metu."

— Terence, *Adelphi*

I know something of the physical nature of bodies — how they are constructed, the gentle architecture of our organs within this scaffold of bones. Blindfolded, I can trace the arteries and muscles that bind these things together, making us whole. I am well trained in my craft, even to mapping the delicate geography which sheathes us all.

There are no mysteries, not anymore — at least, I thought so then.

Once, early in my apprenticeship, my father opened a door in my mind, revealing a wider plane of understanding beyond the physical world we worked so diligently to serve.

I was very young and, bringing one of my textbooks to him, I pointed to a word that had perplexed me. Rather than direct me to a dictionary to find out on my own, he couldn't resist an opportunity to breathe life into that dry definition for me.

The word was *integrity* and this is what he said...

"Do you know what it means when we say something is integrated? All of it's parts fit together, each function complementing the function of the others — nothing wasted, nothing left out, nothing misplaced. We say that these things are integrated together — fused for one purpose.

"Now, when we say that a man has integrity we're speaking of more than just his physical body. We're saying something important about his entire being — his body, mind, and his soul. Each behaves interdependently, muscle moves against muscle to propel him forward throughout his life's journey. He joins his beliefs to his mind, his mind to his body, and finally his body is wed to his actions which demonstrate his beliefs. Even the simplest gesture — the passing of a hand across his eyes, for example — can reveal the foundation upon which his soul is built. When a man follows the boundaries drawn by his guiding beliefs, we say that he walks with integrity. For he is *integrated*, do you see?"

I was still rather young for this sort of thinking. "But . . . if someone is evil and does evil things . . . then does that mean he has integrity?"

My father nodded. "After a fashion, for his actions truly follow his spirit. But his evil makes an exile of himself from something larger still."

He led me over to the door of the masonshack and pointed out into the fields beyond. "Look around you. Everything has been brought together by the hand of God, placed not in some random, haphazard fashion, but with careful design and clear purpose which only He alone can see."

Out in the graveyard, I saw Mason — a much younger, heartier man at the time — digging a grave.

My father did not need to point to him when he said "There is true integrity."

CHAPTER EIGHT

"Margaret Sojourner Lewis, aged thirty-seven, stands today accused of indecent contact and immoral, morbid congress. It is the opinion of this righteous prefecture that, since she chose to love death, Miss Lewis should be wed to her lover at dawn tomorrow, drawn together in the happy circle of the hangman's noose."

— From *The Annotated Whitehall Trial Transcripts of 1863*
by Wilson Belding

I often think of my father's words when I visit the village. The people there make such an effort to maintain the outward perception of piety which only serves as little more than a thin shell of propriety around their daily lives. And they try harder with none other than myself, as though they can blind my eyes to the final evidence of all of their secrets, each one leaving an indelible mark just beneath their carefully cultivated facade. The blackened liver of the teetotaler, the diseased pudenda of the prude — whatever your secrets, your undertaker shall uncover them in the end.

There was a time when I believed that integrity could only be achieved in solitude; that the act of participating within a community of any size led to a mind of fractured loyalties brought about by the attempt to accommodate opposing positions and decisions. And so, by extension, I fancied my own solitude as proof positive of a strong personal integrity well established beyond that of my neighbors.

I am old enough now to know how wrong, how arrogant I was.

Outside of town, I stopped at the Western gate and rapped lightly on the watchman's door. I heard him stir within and throw the bolt. His bleary eyes peered out of the inner darkness, nodded silently in recognition before closing the door once more. Like most others, he did not care to linger long in conversation with me. I waited as his muffled footfalls rose to the meager height of his rickety tower where the bell rang and then once more.

I could hear him wheezing as he descended. Once more, he drew the bolt to peer out at me and nod. His face was flushed. Soon enough, I thought, the council would need to elect a new watchman for the impending and, to my experienced eye, obvious vacancy.

With the warning sounded, permission granted, and formality of custom complete, I entered the village.

As I made my way into town, I saw a few men here and there: Merchants readying their custom for the day, laborers on their way to their employment. I nodded to them and they touched their caps. Their relief as I passed was palpable, as though I was the harbinger of Death and not merely her custodian. And, of course, the watchmen's tolling bell ensured that I would encounter no women, nor they me.

Each year, the winter season drains the village gray, leaching it of life. The drab stone and wood buildings cluster around a central square, creating a haphazard maze of lanes and alleys radiating outward. Every structure gives the impression that it might fall down at any moment, the stained and dreary walls sagging under the weight of the slate roofs, settling against each other like companion drunkards staggering home after the public house has closed for the night.

Once, I imagine, the village must have been new. And yet it has been this way since I can remember. For all I know, the village will always perch on the edge of decay without collapsing. Perhaps, in founding the town, my family cursed it to remain in this perpetual condition on the borders of life as well.

Spring and summer eventually bring some color, some warmth — but not enough to adequately explain why anyone elects to reside here. Whatever industry or opportunity inspired my family to establish the original settlement, it has long since faded away, leaving naught but the fundamentals of living and dying. As such, my position is perhaps the most secure in the community. We will always have our dead.

Despite the troubled times brought on by the lingering gloom of winter, I felt oddly optimistic that day. My spirits had lightened somewhat, struggling free from the shadow of the previous few days. It might have been the prospect of a visit to Burke's shop, or perhaps the faint yet unmistakable cessation of winter.

I cannot say that there was an actual warmth in the air, but at least the cold edge of the season had been dulled somewhat. The overcast sky looked thin to my eyes, bruised from the outside, as though at any moment the sun might finally and at long last batter through to reach us once more.

And so, when I heard the faint voice above, I glanced up without a thought.

A woman stood on a small balcony, tending to a clothesline strung between the two drab buildings that rose on either side of me. As she worked, she hummed softly under her breath — her voice so light, I scarce could hear it on the wind.

The pale morning light fixed her for a moment in my gaze, in my memory forever: Her hair coming undone in the wind, the cock of her broad hips supporting the weight of the basket she held with one hand while she plucked out laundry to hang with the other . . . her frank and open face gazing down at me.

She should have gone inside, should have put custom ahead of her chores. But she had not.

Perhaps she was in a hurry, too busy to bow to ceremony and superstition or too defiant. Perhaps she was curious. Perhaps she did not recognize me there in the shadow between the two buildings.

And perhaps I was not mistaken when I thought that, catching my eye, I saw her smile.

In that moment, there was nothing that I wanted more than to climb those steps two at a time and take her in my arms, breathe in the smell of her skin, plunge my hands into her hair, turn my neck to her lips...

It was a moment, an impulse. It passed.

I walked on and I did not dare look up again.

Though I continued to visit to the village regularly throughout the intervening years, I would not pass that way again. I do not know if that is a sign of integrity or not.

I wonder what my father would say?

I wonder if I will recognize her when she is brought to me?

I wonder if the one who tends to my forgotten flesh will see some faint clue pointing to that moment which I have hidden, have treasured for so long.

It was a moment, an impulse. It passed.

More likely it will be Burke who uncovers my secret — picking over the remnants of my life, selecting the trinkets worth saving and relegating the rest to the junk heap. Perhaps he will find this thin remembrance among my books, poring over my tale and pausing for a moment when he discovers this, my solitary heresy and my rarest shame . . . or perhaps my autobiographical efforts will be eclipsed by the massive wealth of the rest of my library.

I imagine that it will feel something like a family reunion for Burke, since I obtained much of my library from his shop. He never let a book go without a wistful struggle, not even to me. The reconciliation with those prodigals might even dull the edge of whatever sorrow he feels at my passing.

Not that he will not mourn, I know. My weekly trips into the village, those businesslike visits are little more than pretext that I might visit his shop. Burke and I long ago recognized each other as kindred, a species shared and unique among the dull minds of the village. They see an unplowed field, measuring its value by the meter and going no deeper than inches into the soil teeming with mysterious poetry. Every weekday a drudgery, every weeknight a binge, and every Sabbath a hypocrisy. They subsist on the petty gossip of the tavern and the market square — while Burke and I, we eavesdrop on the whispers of God.

Burke is no dull native. He came out of the broader world to settle here, he says, to live a life of contemplation and reflection among the simple, honest folk — those same who, within a few years, had robbed him blind. "Outsider prices" is what they called it, what they still call it. Even now, fifteen years on, Burke remains the stranger.

"Only now," as the maxim goes, "He knows when to trust a coin and when to use his teeth."

I do not know what brought him here, but I know it was not the lure of the simple life. He would not have lasted a week unless he'd some other purpose to stay among those so unwelcoming, so corrupt. Whether it was misfortune that drove him to this exile or if he fled some misdeed of his own, regardless of the cause, he soon found himself marooned and unable to return even if he had desired it. Near penniless, he discovered a secret revenue to sustain him, making the most of the innate qualities of those same villagers who had bled him white.

On the surface, the village was simplicity itself. Yet below the dull skin, this pond swarmed with black tangles of resentment upon which poisonous minds fed. The long heritage of the village had led to countless little slights, disagreements, and outright swindles over the years.

As such: Twenty years before his death, the butcher might have accepted an heirloom brooch in payment for an overdue marker held by the blacksmith. The story told to the blacksmith's children had, over the years, raised the value of the heirloom quite considerably in their eyes. And in the recitation, so also grew the unfair usury of the villainous butcher — a perhaps-undeserved reputation he would take to his grave, that selfsame plot upon which the blacksmith's children finally danced.

It was Burke who came then to the butcher's wife, offering his sympathies and appropriate comforts. In confidence he revealed to her his plans to open a small shop. He was seeking merchandise, seed corn with which to start this venture. The butcher had been a man of taste, a collector even. Perhaps Burke could inspect the estate and help ease the loss by purchasing any items upon which her sentiment was not attached?

The butcher's wife, bereft of her husband's income, might have allowed for such a possibility. Perhaps she hoped for kinder comforts in addition to the fresh faced outsider's money. Her husband had not been a man of gentle deportment and she was twenty-five years his junior. No matter, she'd not married him for love. She would not complicate the comfort of the brute's passing with mournful pretense.

And to the blacksmith's children, Burke soon offered them restitution on their long-standing grudge. Grateful and triumphant, they paid his asking price and celebrated the return of the prodigal brooch.

The week the butcher died, died also six more inhabitants of our little community. It was a windfall time for my trade as well as Burke's. Our paths crossed often as we provided our partner services to those seven families — he tidying up the castoffs from those lives while I collected the lives themselves. We recognized each other, the resemblance and the irony: His was a comforting presence welcome in their homes, while I was viewed to be a ghoul feeding on their grief.

I noted the literary references with which he so liberally seasoned his conversation. And he saw my comprehension as a spark of light within the dark thicket of dull minds surrounding him. It was not long before our friendship was secure.

As was his business. In time, the villagers began to establish consignments with him in anticipation of their passing with the proceeds guaranteed to their heirs — minus his own generous commission, of course. Burke's shop swelled with curios and antiquities. He made his living in barter as much as he did in coin. In the intervening years, he had sifted the petty grievances and paltry heirlooms of their lives many times over, long surpassing the original "investment" he'd made in the village. Often I wondered if that had not been his plan all along.

Nor am I immune to the appeal of his shop. Every piece of merchandise has a story to tell and Burke delights in recounting the arcane and often scandalous history. I think I must represent a safe outlet for these tales, one with whom he is safe to be indiscreet in revealing the weaknesses of the village and his craft in exploiting them. I sometimes wonder how he gains such insight into these lives.

That Burke has a way about him, there is no doubt. And I have no doubt that the butcher's wife, among others, would agree.

All the more reason why I look forward to my weekly visits to his shop, though my tastes do not run typical of his customers. I live a austere life and the stories he shares are far more interesting to me than the objects that inspired them. I have no need to purchase someone else's squandered heirlooms.

Yet, of course, there are the books. Self-imposed or no, Burke's exile from the wider world does not extend to the shipments that arrive on the monthly coach. The crates that bear his name are packed with rare literary delicacies and he is a glutton. From the popular fictions of the day to the aged and crumbling relics of the past century, Burke gathers the books all to himself, prowling among them and devouring all in his eternal, cyclopean hunger.

From his clutches I rescue what few I can afford. Were it not for the alignment of our natures, I suspect that he would refuse to part with his captives at all. Unlike his other merchandise, he does everything he can to discourage a customer's interest in his books. His solution to the rare inquiry from one of the other villagers is ingenious: To those that he must oblige, that cannot be put off any other way, he sets a price so high, so ridiculous that few of them ever consider matching.

I have long chided him for this. It is one thing to complain about the dimness of your neighbors. It is quite another to actively discourage them from expanding their understanding. His retort is that an enthusiasm for cheap romance, melodramatic suspense, and tea party theology does not necessarily indicate a disposition inclined to embrace a broader perspective of the world.

I protest that he reads those common, popular books as well — but Burke is never one to be caught in a contradiction. He reminds me that a limited, confectionery diet conditions a palate so that it is no more sophisticated than that of a child's. The wholesome is spat out, shunned in favor of immature tastes. Unlike his prospective customers, Burke has no such limits.

"Besides," he tells me. "Any merchant worth his salt takes the time to know his product and that of his competition."

And so Burke manages to keep most of his precious library, more or less, out of those enthusiastic (albeit ignorant) hands — though not out of mine.

The familiar squeal of the door to his shop sounds under my hand as I enter. Burke long ago removed the bell in deference to the traditions of my office. Most others of the merchant caste in my village are not so accommodating. I must knock and wait to be admitted, rather than let the bell ring.

Burke's shop overflows with merchandise from castoff lives all tumbled together. Coming from the contained order of my world, the haphazard maze of aisles and shelves always leaves me a little overwhelmed and, I confess, a little thrilled as well. Each visit to the shop is different from the previous ones. I could spend — and have spent — hours picking through the shelves with no sense of ever coming to the end. New discoveries wait everywhere my eye falls. Nothing is ever the same from visit to visit. It is almost as if Burke empties the shop each time I leave, repopulating it with a whole new stock before I return.

At times, shopping there is like trying to practice archaeology on top of an avalanche in progress.

Once, I made a pact with myself that I would remember one single thing, one object and where it was located in the shop. I picked a small ball of hand-blown glass that rested on a shelf, propping up a collection of cheap pasteboard bound novellas. It was a very lovely object, though dusty, about the size of a large grapefruit — hollow and shot through with threads of glass within. I left it where I found it and made a careful notation in my memory of where it was in the shelves.

The following week when I returned, I made my way to the very spot but found nothing familiar. The glass ball had gone, along with the pasteboard bound books and even the shelf itself. I strolled through the store and saw that one or two of the pastes had been relocated . . . but there was no sign of the ball.

When I asked Burke about it, he professed ignorance. I suspect he reconfigures his store at a whim. Perhaps it creates a sense of urgency in the customer's mind. If you never know if the thing you desire is going to be there when you return, you are more likely to make a purchase on the spot.

In my case, it is an effective tactic. I typically take my time as I browse, keeping my eyes open for books stuffed here and there among his merchandise. If ever I find anything of interest, I waste no time in snatching it up lest it should vanish immediately. By the time I reach Burke, I usually have four or five purchases tucked under my arm. I am ashamed to admit that sometimes I might have five times that many, if Burke has had a good shipment that week.

He sits at a high table near the back of the store, surrounded by all of his merchandise like a stone idol staring down upon its burnt offerings. The table serves as his counter and his altar. He makes change out of an old cigar box he keeps to one side.

He once confided to me that he configured the aisles of the store so that he could stay at the table and keep watch over every customer from this single point of observation. "Like your God, eh?" He smiles as he says it, in case I might be offended (I am not). "Keeping watch over the Dominion."

"He keeps watch over the borders," I cannot help but correct him. "We are the caretakers of the creation within."

Burke shrugs, no interest in theology. "Well, I can't let everyone rob me blind."

I find I have strayed from my narrative and gone wandering in Burke's shop — and not for the first time.

No, I was writing of that one day, when I stood on the cusp of spring with the winter at my back and the washer woman still humming in my mind.

The familiar squeal of the door to his shop sounds under my hand as I enter. From deep within the store, I hear Burke's voice rumble ominous, characteristically melodramatic: "Enter freely and of your own will."

I do so, letting the door swing gently closed behind me before I wade into his chaos, doing my best to keep my head above the surface as I scan the shelves.

I have no interest in Burke's main trade. I am no collector of junk store remnants nor antiquities. But there *are* books. Each new discovery, tucked away here and there, is a seduction . . . a revelation.

By the time I have found Burke at the center of his maze, my arms are heavy with selections. I unload them on his table and, as I always do, I tell him that he will be the ruin of me. He nods, inspecting my treasures with a critical eye.

"Ornithology?" His eyebrow, already cocked, arches even higher. "'When the wind is southerly...'" he mutters, flipping through the tombstone-sized encyclopedia in front of him. "Taking up a new hobby, are we? Or just need the fresh air?"

I mumble something about nocturnal egrets.

Burke snorts. "Sounds more like nightmares to me." He taps the stack of books in front of him, nodding.

"Which reminds me," he says, rising and backing away into the bowels of the shop. I wait until he once again appears, from a completely different direction than from the way he left. He carries a parcel wrapped in brown paper, laying it gently on the tabletop between us.

"I can't make heads or tails of these," he tells me as he tears away the paper. "But they're lovely and," his voice lowers slightly as he leans in. "I suspect they're quite rare."

Lovely is the word for them, yes. Not the cheap pasteboards that litter his shop, but something far more elegant. I take each of the books as he draws them out, running my fingers over the embroidered silk covers, tracing the vague characters stitched into the bindings with golden and scarlet thread. Each book opens with a sigh, my fingertips hot as they spread the thin rice paper leaves. Inky dragons and birds glide across my eyes as I stroke the books.

There are five in all and I cannot help but give Burke a grateful, shuddering look as I close the last of them. It is a long moment indeed before I can remember to ask "Where did you find these?"

48

"Well, I'm not sure," Burke gives me the smile that every brothel keeper is born with. "Let me think for a moment..."

I wait. This is his game now and I do not mind playing it, so long as I get these books when I go.

"Yes," he says at last. "These are new arrivals, just this week. They belonged to that boy, the dead boy."

My hands stop caressing the books. I raise my eyes to his.

He meets my gaze. "Cires Ling's son."

I nod. "Yes. I buried him."

Burke grunts. "So I heard. There was some squawking from Hampton and the other merchant magpies about it."

"Regarding?" If I am curt, he knows it is not with him.

The answer shrugs its way out of him. "Some of them didn't like the idea of it."

I shake my head. I do not follow his point.

He gives me a look, striking to the heart of the matter. "They weren't overly thrilled to hear a foreigner got planted in 'their' graveyard, a pagan and idolater sharing holy dirt with the true believers. Hampton was, as usual, the ringleader."

Hampton. The local tobacconist and chief Pharisee is not one of my favorites — unfortunately, and to my deep regret, a visit to his shop is another of my errands to be made this day.

"Do tell?" I ask quietly, my hand drifting across the books, fingers touching them lightly. I won't be able to resist them, I know, once I get them home.

Burke sighs. He has even less tolerance than I for those who profess and profane faith with the same breath. "'Ingratia patria, ne ossa quidem habebis.'"

I nod, only half listening, wondering if thinly veiled prejudice was enough motivation to inspire a group of overweight, pompous sluggards to defile a grave . . . wondering if the pious inhabitants of the village were wretched enough to rouse themselves for that.

I thought they might be, just.

"Strange books for a boy," he says, turning one of the elegant volumes over in his hands "Even a dead one."

I shrug. It would not be the first time I'd purchased a dead man's books. As I've said, Burke was my chief procurer. I suppose with my own passing that, if he still maintains an active business, he will be delighted to absorb my rather extensive library once more — though, I expect he'll have some trouble accommodating it all as his shelves are already sagging. He'll certainly have trouble selling any of it, given the contemporary tastes. I am, as they say, old school.

"I'm amazed she gave these up." He runs his fingers over one of them, faint gold and turquoise threadwork decorating the cover. "Rare as they are, since she stopped writing."

"How do you mean?"

He looks at me with pantomime incredulity. "You mean you don't know her?"

I don't and I tell him so.

"My gods . . . Cires Ling? The author?"

I shake my head. Burke's penchant for the dramatic sometimes irritates me. Like many who have drifted into the borderlands of obesity, his enthusiasms and mannerisms are so childlike and delicate — oddly effeminate, even — that they strike a grotesque chord in comparison to the massivity of the rest of his figure. At times, it can be tiresome to fix my attention on such an odd balance of opposites.

Burke gently returns the book to the company of its companions, folding the brown paper over them as light and loving as a mother swaddling her newborn babe.

And, filling the expanse of his lungs with the breath required to begin his tale, he begins to speak.

CHAPTER NINE

"I have heard the lies, yes... I have heard them and I believe them all."

— Charles Fairchild, *Windfallen*

"Cires Ling? The things I've heard about her, the stories and gossip and rumors? Well, it's just fortunate that the folks around here don't know anything about her past . . . They wouldn't just cheat her and whisper behind her back, they'd burn her house down."

His words reopen the grave in my mind.

"And to top it all off, they say she was the reason that Gaines killed himself. I've half a mind to burn her house down myself, for all of that."

I shake my head, only a few steps down the meandering path of his story and already he's gotten me quite lost. "Gaines?"

"Michel-Robert Gaines? The writer?" He shakes his head at me. "And you say you know books."

I have never said so, but he continues on regardless.

"They say she was his mistress and, from the gossip, it seems that he was far more passionate for her than she for him. It's quote common knowledge that he wrote 'Bottle of Shadows' about her — *for* her, really. Most of his major stories got their start in her eyes."

I nod, less interested than I feign for Burke's sake. I remembered Gaines somewhat now. And I recalled that I didn't care for his writing, though he'd been one of the leading novelists of his time. I vaguely recalled some mention of suicide on the flyleaf of his final book. I'd read it on the recommendation of a classmate at the Academy.

It was not my cup of tea, to say the least.

Though he'd made his name as a romantic fantasist, Gaines dipped into darker and somewhat distasteful waters during his latter years. The lead character of his final work — a book finished just weeks before he took his own life, as I recalled — is consumed by a succubus, drained of his soul drop by drop, until only a husk remains.

The book disturbed me intensely. Had I not already offered my allegiance to the rigorous strictures of my office, I have no doubt that the story would have instilled in me an insurmountable aversion to the female sex as a whole.

Gaines was an old name in my mind, a forgotten detail from my student years. Secondhand gossip about his romantic entanglements could not possibly interest me less.

Burke, however, reveled in it all. "And . . . when she was done with him, she tossed him aside without a second thought. Or so they say."

He played his fingertips lightly over the paper parcel, tapping out his words as deliberately as any author at their typograph. "She wrote these books here but that just scratches the surface. I've heard that she has over a thousand stories to her name."

A thousand stories seemed unlikely for anyone's career, however advanced in years or gifted with talent and productivity.

"A thousand *stories*," Burke assures me. "She wrote in the tradition of her celestial forbears, galvanizing the Eastern mythologies with her own contemporary style. She was, in her own way, a sensation."

I question whether quality might suffer under the weight of such quantity of output.

"Don't you even suggest it." Burke dismisses the question before I can finish framing it. "Everyone who has read her work says it's masterful. Would that I could claim to be one of them."

I cannot help but look to the stack of volumes in front of him.

Pityingly, he hands it to me.

I leaf through it again, my understanding clearing as he continues.

"Ling hasn't written in our language — and won't, so she says. Our barbarous tongue is far too blunt and crude to shape the elegance of her style. 'Le tranductions augmentent les faultes dun ouvrage et en gâtent les beautés.'"

I recognize the reference despite his atrocious pronunciation. But I am unable to determine whether or not he speaks with admiration or mockery of her views.

"As it is, her books have only seen print overseas and the most avid collectors," here he bows his modest head, "Will pay through the nose for them. They say that no one has managed to gather a complete set of her comprehensive works but," he says, the brown paper rustling under his fingertips, "This will certainly get me started . . . unless, of course, you're interested?"

I wonder, briefly, if he's putting on this show to sweeten his sale. It may not matter as, apparently, I am interested enough to ask further after the books.

The volume I hold in my hand is a fascinating mix of incomprehensible Asiatic characters and ink brush illustrations. It is lovely and the mystery of it recalls to me those eyes behind the veil.

I itch to own them all. I do my best to hide this from him.

Burke, pantomime nonchalant, shrugs. "Supposedly they're lovely tales. According to the catalogs, full of fantasy and magic. Princesses and dragons and curses — that's the sort of thing she wrote about. They might only be fairy stories, but people say she puts everyone else in the pale. Of course, you'd have to learn the language if you ever wanted to read one of them."

I did. I wanted to read all of them.

I was not — I am not — a collector, after all. I am an addict.

Burke fans the books out before him, the silk bindings glimmering in the dim light of his shop.

"She's stopped writing, of course. Her last novel was so . . . influential that she had to come to this country to escape what she had stirred up in her own."

I wait, knowing he can't help himself but continue.

"Apparently, a portion of her readership became rather hysterical."

I cannot hide my skepticism. "Over a fairy tale?"

"This time, Cires Ling dipped her pen in horror. Tired of princesses and maidens, she sought to sharpen her teeth on monsters instead. From what I've heard, that last book dealt with subjects taboo in *any* culture, something to do with witchcraft or sorcery — worse, even."

He shakes his head. "As I've heard it, people went somewhat mad with it all. There were unsavory rumors of readers going around opening throats, blood rituals . . . perhaps even worse besides. It was all hideous, I understand. But there must have been something powerful in her writing for people to behave that way."

I press him for more about the book itself.

"The novel was a story of a family cursed, the firstborn children disfigured in some distasteful manner. There's always a curse in their stories, of course. Their culture thrives on them. And, of course, they say *we're* the barbarians."

"And the story?"

"As I said, it's a horror story — a novelette, really — one of the shortest things she ever wrote. But it was long enough that people were either clamoring for her blood or living by her book like it was holy writ. Quite by accident, her little dalliance in the macabre sparked something quite like a civil war. The church — *their* church, of course — excommunicated her. And she was forbidden by that Iron Hand government of theirs from ever writing again."

Strange as it seems now, such censorship was not uncommon in those times. Even the relatively permissive attitude of our own Ministry would, from time to time, provide gentle guidance to the authors and artists of the United Dominion. Such passive involvement paled in comparison to the purges and pogroms acted out by the Iron Hand upon its own peoples.

"So . . . long story short, she left for good, forever."

"Does she continue to write? Is she writing still?"

Burke shrugs again, with finality. "She refuses to write in our language and none of the publishers in her own country will consider her, for fear of reprisals from the Hand — or, worse still, another civil outbreak of madness inspired by her works."

He grins at me, wry and sour. "So you can only imagine, what Hampton and the others would have to say if they got their teeth into the meat of her story."

Too well, yes, I could imagine.

"As it is, the tilt of those eyes, the strange music of her voice..." he shakes his head. "That's enough as it is, for them to justify their treatment of her."

His sigh betrays thoughts so similar to my own. I tamp down the embers of my jealousy. I am no schoolboy.

Burke shakes his head. "I can only imagine what they'd do if they knew her history . . . let alone read these books."

I look down at the small treasure arrayed before me and I recite the creed every addict knows by heart: I cannot afford them. I do not need them. I must have them.

Burke, of course, knows all of this better than I myself. "So you be careful with these rarities. I don't know why she would even bother entrusting them to you, but there it is."

I open my mouth and then close it again.

He chuckles. "They're yours. She left them here for you. I wasn't supposed to tell, but..." he shrugs. "Whatever it was, you made an impression."

The gears of my mind work over all of this. "But . . . I only met her briefly, just a moment or two, and not in the best of circumstances."

She left them for me, I tell myself.

"Don't get too impressed," he says. "I wouldn't want the damned things in my shop for long. It's all right for you, so far out of town. Some of us are within striking distance."

"But why leave these for me? What did she say?"

He shakes his head. "She didn't say, not exactly. I had the impression you'd done her a favor and she was grateful. It was hard to understand her though, through the veil."

"She came here herself?"

Burke does not smile now. He does not need to. "Of course."

I turn the parcel over in my hands, baffled by the gift.

"What was it called?" I wonder aloud. "That last book, is it one of these?"

"How would I know? I didn't think to ask until after she'd gone. But it's called 'The Monster' or possibly 'The Dragon'. The few critics in this country who've read it disagree on the title. It's the rarest of all her published works. Most of the copies were confiscated by the Hand. They're not opposed to an old fashioned bonfire, when the season is right."

"You mentioned something about a curse?"

Burke looks away before he answers, making a show of drawing up a receipt for my other purchases. "As I understand it . . . the story tells of a burning thirst, a necessity to subsist on living blood for survival."

I wonder silently how someone so beautiful could bring something so horrible to life?

My question unanswerable, I pay for my books — though Burke refused payment for those my Eastern neighbor left for me — and head out to see to my other errands, impatient to return home so I can enjoy my unexpected boon.

Burke, for once, seems relieved to see me go.

CHAPTER TEN

"The dismal practitioner must, at all times, recall to himself his role as servant to the community. The temptation for over-familiarity, even friendship, must be resisted. To bear the burden of so many sorrows is counter to the duties of your office. Likewise, it is extremely bad for business."

— from *The Personal Correspondence of Thomas Harvey Nichols, Executioner*

Hampton — our local tobacconist — draws at each breath the way a newborn suckles, in a desperate effort to drag himself across the boundary of life and death. And when he exhales, it is as if his entire frame were forcing the grudging ethereal gasses out in some strange exorcism of oxygen.

I dread visiting his establishment and, if not for his special blend tobaccos, I doubt I would choose to indulge in his presence at all. Stepping into his shop should be a peaceful, luxuriant experience. The dark warm pungency of his wares drifting in the air around me, I want to close my eyes and give myself over to burial in that dark rich soil.

But the initial moment of peace is always broken by Hampton's locomotive approach up the main aisle, snuffling and puffing as he greets me with the fatuous grimace that serves as his only smile.

My hand pumped to numbness, he wipes his palm on that perpetual apron of his — an unconscious gesture, I assume, to remove any lingering taint of death our brief contact might have left behind — and bids me to enter, making his customary apologies for my order being "Not quite ready, as such" as he charges down the aisle to his work table at the back of the shop.

I nod and grind my teeth. The purchase is a standing order, which I collect on the same day every week. It would not challenge him to prepare it ahead of my arrival — but then he would not have the pleasure of battering me with his erudite observations and questions while I wait.

Hampton's beliefs had long plagued me with irritation. I begrudge no man the security of his faith but his annoyed me for the simple fact that, at a fundamental level, his philosophy ran parallel to my own. The irritation lay in Hampton's singular ability to not only express our shared beliefs rather poorly, but also managing to justify them for entirely the wrong reasons.

Hampton was a child, dissecting a hummingbird to expose the clockwork he asserted must be there — for does it not move, does it not buzz? Such was his logical progression.

There is nothing so irritating as being forced to admit agreement with a man you believe to be an utter fool in all other matters.

And, more salt in the wound, he called me "Reverend" when he knew full well that my office has no formal theological certification nor do I carry the weight of ordination. But that did not discourage him from assigning to me a lofty title equal to his own vanity, whether I deserved it or not.

I left him to babble away in the back of the shop while I browsed the racks and shelves of jars, each filled with such rich aromas.

Common cigarettes were not to be found among his stock, as Hampton considered them a feeble, bastard product of foreign lands. Moreover, in comparison to his own aromatic delicacies, cigarettes stank — my own, of course, being the only exception to this as they were of his own manufacture. He protected his vanity by wrapping my fags in darker, treated papers rather than the common white wrapped smokes of the working classes.

I had discovered the art of tobacco when I'd been away at school. Despite Hampton's vain elevation, my own profession was of the working class, after all — and I'd become sufficiently accustomed to cigarettes, so much so that I was somewhat reluctant to give over the habit once I'd returned home. As it has been admitted, I am an addict at my core.

Despite Hampton's periodic pleadings, I would not consider a pipe. I was, I felt, far too young for such an affectation and pipes had always struck me as fussy things, less meant for enjoyment than as something with which one could occupy his hands during awkward conversational lulls. Not even Hampton had driven me to that, not as yet.

But he accepted my new vice eventually, working for days to produce the proper blend of tobaccos and spices wrapped in dark papers soaked in clove oil. Despite his other failings, the man was a master of his craft and my weekly visits were secured after the first sample of his new, exclusive blend. Not even his insistence to refer to them as "cigarillos" would dissuade me from placing a standing order.

In his shop that day, I ran my fingers over the various jars and considered giving up my vice altogether — as I had done every week for time out of mind. Not for my health, no, but because of my irritation with Hampton himself. One day I would finally succumb to my impulses and, I feared, take out ten years of my silent disagreement and frustration on him. He was, I have no doubt, blithely unaware of my dislike. I suspect he even thought us to be friends.

Behind me, Hampton's voice rose and gained shape as he returned, still talking. I gathered that he'd just finished up a rather long-winded (even for him) diatribe on one of his favorite topics, specifically the inferiority of all things foreign.

He stared at me, puffing and earnest, holding out a parcel in his hands. His eagerness to please, his desire to secure my good will and agreement, only further increased my dislike of the man and I tried hard to keep these things submerged beneath a placid, albeit bland, expression.

Guilt overtook me, as it so often did. I had to believe that what lay at the core of his soul was good, even if it had been encased over the years in material far more suspect. But he was, beneath the gasping meatiness of him, a good hearted man.

I realized that he was waiting for my response to some comment I'd not heard.

I nodded vaguely, hoping that I was not agreeing to anything more egregious than his typical idiocy, reaching to take my order from him.

Hampton however, retained a grip on his little hostages and stared me down with eyes that had gradually gone yellow over the years, like the meat of a fresh sliced apple rotting in the air. "Why then, Reverend Plinge, would you allow them to set down roots, as it were?"

His voice had an unusual, accusatory tone to it — almost surly and certainly not his typical, deferential manner.

"I don't quite follow you," I replied, desperately trying to recall his last comments. What had he said, something about foreigners?

He snuffled, vaguely righteous and indignant. "Why would someone such as them bury a child so far from their own land, unless they had no plans to return?"

Cires Ling, I thought. *He's talking about Cires Ling.*

My mind cast back to the muddy footprints around her poor son's gravesite desecrated for no other reason than that she was an outsider. It occurred to me that the quality of exile forced upon me by my position might lie at the heart of the sympathy I felt for her.

"Why would you allow them, Reverend? It's not their land, it's ours. And they defiled it with their unholy rituals, their false gods. There's some that have been saying that the likes of those shouldn't be putting their dead in our dirt, and that you ought not to have allowed it."

The mingled anger and hurt in his yellowed eyes infuriated me. Would that I could say that my response was born of fatigue after so busy a season, that it has not been my intention to lace my words with such venom. But the truth of it is that I had harbored similar concerns, choosing the conscience of my office over that of my heart. Confronted by Hampton's ignorance and prejudice — and perhaps ashamed of my own — I bristled immediately.

"If it is any comfort, you are not alone in your opinions." I said coolly.

He nodded at this. I could tell that he expected me to agree with him. He grimaced broadly in satisfaction, the closest approximation to a smile I had ever seen him present. I cut him off before he could respond.

"Indeed, I could not tell you who for I do not myself know. But at least one person in this blessed little village of ours not only shares your opinion that the boy does not belong in our graveyard, they went so far as to attempt to expel him from it."

His eyes narrowed and he sniffed, uncertain. "How do you mean, Reverend?"

"I mean that some fine, upstanding members of our holy little parish stole into the graveyard last evening and attempted to dig up the poor child, disturbing the rest that Death had seen fit to bestow upon him."

"Who?" His surprise struck me as affected and I assumed that he must have known about the event, if not participated in it himself.

"I don't pretend to know, Hampton, but it happened all the same. And when the watchdog caught them in the act, they gutted the poor animal, leaving her carcass for Mason to discover."

Hampton gobbled in surprise at that last twist of the knife. Mason was well liked in the community. He spent his day off each week in the Veterans' Hall, playing checkers with the rest of the old duffers, including Hampton.

In my rage, I had the presence of mind enough to realize that Hampton could not have done such an act. He was an ass, but he was not so cruel. Whatever he knew about the vandalism, it was unlikely he'd been directly involved.

But still, he'd known — or, at least, he'd heard about it after the fact. I had no doubt. I slapped my hand down, rattling the jars down the length of the counter top and noting with satisfaction that Hampton's eyes widened.

"You tell them," I ground the words between my teeth. "You tell them when next you see them at the Sabbath Lodge after your sham, pious services . . . tell them that I received their message. Kindly deliver to them my response: Go to Hell."

"Reverend!"

It was all I could do not to slap him. "Leave off the hollow honorifics, you fat hypocrite. The commission I have is not a holy one, but the office I serve *is*. The graveyard has been in the care of my family for five generations. We were the first ones here and one day we'll bury you all before we move on."

I leaned in close to him. "Except for those bastards that dug my dirt last night. I'll not bury them. I'll see that they rot above the ground. If my dirt is too good for that poor, doomed boy, then it's *certainly* too good for them. Terminus sees more than you think, Hampton. God is not mocked, and your friends will die knowing it. Tell them that."

He nodded, a small bubble forming at one nostril, undulating with fear.

It popped and my anger dissipated.

Hampton wasn't the sort to go into the fields at night with a shovel over his shoulder. Of all his miserable qualities — mutterer, racist, hypocrite — he was no vandal. He'd gossip all day long, but he'd never act. The craven, petty man before me wasn't even worth the effort I'd put into my indignation. I'm ashamed of it, even now.

Wearily, I turned and left his shop without another word.

I was only a few streets away when I realized that I'd left my cigarettes behind. After my lapse of temper, I hadn't the stomach to return for them. It was going to be a long walk home without their comfort.

The watchman rang the bell as I passed back through the gates of the village. And not for the last time did I think of the washer woman so content on her balcony.

Had she seen me, had she known me?

The bell rang again at my back, releasing the village from their confinement.

I shook my head, a bitter taste filling my mouth at the sound.

They ought to fear hypocrisy more than heresy.

CHAPTER ELEVEN

"Death and the sun are not to be looked at in the face."

— from *The Maxims of La Rochefoucauld*

My regret weighed heavy on me during my walk home

Regardless of his culpability, Hampton was, at best, an inveterate gossip. I had no doubt that by the time I reached my own gate, those responsible for the vandalism in the yard would have the news of my outburst along with the rest of the village, of course.

Steeped in frustration, I berated myself at each step for giving them the satisfaction. I wished, profoundly, that I had not gone into town that morning but stayed behind to tend the graveyard with Mason.

Had I not, though, it would have made little difference to anyone but the bluebottles.

I heard them at their work as I made my way through the plots, their cheerful productivity buzzing just beneath the surface of my preoccupied mind.

As it was a cool day, there was little stench.

So it was by sight that I discovered the corpse, already swarming with flies.

I might have said his name, I do not recall.

Regardless, Mason could not answer through that dark veil fluttering and buzzing over his face.

Chapter Twelve

"Who summoned you,
darkest flower?
You are attended by death,
your lips bear the heavy tang of blood.
This vengeance, sister,
this trespass
will not free your heart to love."

— from *Ana's Song* by Michel-Robert Gaines

The house was silent but for the crackling of the dried flowers in the hearth. I held out my hands to their heat but I could not be warmed. The deep fragrance permeated the room with the taste of death and sorrow, so nauseating to me now.

Staring deeply into the embers, I thought of Mason — on the slab, in the box, laying him to rest next to his Lady, whispering the holy rites over him as I tossed shovelfuls of dirt into the hole.

I lay back from the fire. My shoulders ached. Digging a grave is hard work for one to manage alone.

Had he struggled? Had he called out for help? Had he seen the face of his killer or did they take him unawares?

It was with these questions drifting through my mind that I passed over into a most unpleasant dream...

...and it seemed that I was standing in the masonshack with that pale, ruined man laid out before me. I opened him gently with the shears, drawing out his organs one by one. They were shriveled and dried, hollow in my hands.

In the corner of the room, the dog whined, scraping her matted tail across the dusty floor. I threw the parched pieces to her and she snapped them out of the air, popping the leathery scraps between her teeth. She grinned back at me, the cracked tongue lolling out, rasping back and forth against her yellow smile.

Looking back down into Mason's eyes, I searched for some final glimpse of his killer captured in his dull, dry gaze like an insect in amber.

But the only face I found there was my own, darkly warped against his bloodshot eye.

There was a low sound in the room and the dry hinges of the door squealed behind me as I turned...

...and awoke in my library, clenched and taut and chill. The fire burned low in the grate, the familiars dozing restlessly in the corners as they dreamed the dreams of the dead.

I waited there . . . unmoving, listening.

The sound of the door in my nightmare, I felt certain, was an echo of some noise in the waking world pulling me out of my restless dream.

One ear poised against the silent night, I held my breath to listen.

The sound came again, startling in its closeness — a dull rasp, the squeal of wood against wood, from somewhere in the manor above me.

My thoughts immediately went to my sister and I half-rose, not entirely certain of what to do.

She had opened a window, one of the windows facing the graveyard . . . one of those forbidden windows that our ancestor had painted over so many years before.

I feared not for myself but for her. Had it not been forbidden by my office, I would have called out her name. As it was, I could only listen to her voice, low and measured, calling down from above.

And then from below, from outside, a voice replied.

A whispered conversation in the night, their voices loud enough for listening but too soft to be understood. But the meaning was there, the music of it, even without the words.

And so, I could not help but eavesdrop as some unknown suitor romanced my sister by night.

There was so much in his voice as he spoke to her, his words reaching up to catch the gentle rain of her laughter as it fell.

I could not remember the last time I had heard her laugh, that foreign sound filling me with such shame and delight. I imagined her posed like an *ingénue* in one of those modern romances: Her elbows propped on the windowsill, smiling down at her love as he began to sing.

His voice, rising and falling so softly in the night. A sound so pure that I heard her gasp, felt the gentle tug of it myself. It was a song to span the shadows between the stars, to draw them together in a bright and lovely web.

On this went, on he sang to her . . . perhaps for hours. I do not know how long it was before her voice, no more than a whisper, drifted down to him. An invitation, an invocation.

A call from love to love.

I sat back in my chair. Perhaps I was scandalized by her actions, by her disregard for our family's reputation and our name. Perhaps I thought of the woman in the village, her frank and open gaze as she looked down at me.

Perhaps...

I honestly don't remember. But I do recall that my room was cold that long, lonely night and eventually I fell into an envious sleep.

I awoke in the night, the sound of footsteps overhead — measured and rhythmic, moving from one side of the house to the other and then back again. In my mind, I saw the two of them joined together, dancing in each other's arms. I heard their voices mingling in song.

Lulled by their music, I drifted back into sleep only to wake once more much later in the dim hours of the morning — that coldest time — listening as my sister closed her window once more.

Later, off in the fields, that strange animal began to call out once more — the sad and lonely cries breaking the night until morning finally came.

Chapter Thirteen

"Fantasy, abandoned by reason, produces impossible monsters."

— Francisco José de Goya y Lucientes

"Nosferatu," Burke said quietly over his shoulder, leading me through the shop. Around us, the stacked bookshelves seemed to lean in and listen as he continued his litany of names. "Wampyr. Drakul. Leanan-Sídhe. Succubi and Incubi. Prowlers of the night, all undead."

"Undead?" The term was unfamiliar to me.

"Half-human and worse. Hazard's children, the shadows of humanity . . . our darkling cousins."

I nodded curtly. At the moment, I had little patience for Burke's penchant for poetry.

Burke gestured to the books around us. "Inventions all, dreamed up by mothers to keep their children in line . . . stories told around the fire, hunter's tales. Cheap pasteboard diversions. But..."

He stopped at a shelf glancing at the titles. "It is not wise to speak of these old things, my friend. Not even during the day."

He passed a few books to me, adding to the stack I was carrying for him.

I'd come to Burke early that morning with the news of Mason, bearing the mystery of it to him.

Though Mason's wound had been savage, his throat torn to ribbons, there'd been very little blood apart from what soaked through his shredded shirt collar. Had I not known better, I would have said another undertaker had already begun the process of Exsanguination when I'd come across the body.

With more than a month to go before the doddering itinerant prefect for the county would make an appearance, I'd no one to turn to but Burke. I did not know how to investigate nor pursue an assassin. It was obvious to me that the culprit of Lady's demise was responsible for Mason as well. Which ruled out my previous theory; no wolf would have done such a thing and yet left the body unconsumed. And the corpse showed no other signs of struggle.

Burke listened to my curious tale with sympathy and genuine sadness over Mason's murder. His eyes grew sharp when I told him of the loss of blood and the odd cries I'd been hearing in the night. He rattled off that inventory of monsters before we headed off through the shelves. Burke sifted through his stock, handing me volumes to carry as I followed along behind him like a schoolboy.

I walked with him, somewhat disquieted by the small noises around his shop — the creak of the old shelves settling, the sound of books long grown idle.

"Even though these aren't real stories, they might be true," he said at last, somber and thoughtful.

This confused me and I said so.

"Listen to me now: A thing may be true without being real. Think of these books..." he gestured once more to the shop around us. "Full of stories that never happened, populated by people who never lived. And yet each of them has lived as true a story as anything in your life or mine. And with as much substance as either of us, perhaps even more.

"These stories," he told me again, all earnestness. "They may be true."

"But are they real?" I replied.

Frowning, he looked away. "I don't know. All that is, it must grow out of something else. Even lies and fantasies have a kernel of truth at their center. But does that make them real? I don't know."

He nodded, as though convincing himself of the intricacies of his own rationale. "Yes. These stories, they may be real without being true."

Perhaps mistaking my thoughtful silence for confusion, he went on. "What I mean to say is this: If such a monster exists — and I believe that it may — then it is not, it *cannot*, be a true thing. It is a lie of Life that has departed from the living but refuses to wait in the shadow with the rest of the silent dead."

He turned his head at a sudden creak from one of the surrounding shelves — commonplace enough, but it revealed how deep his disquiet ran. For all his philosophical woolgathering and semantics, I understood that Burke was indeed and truly frightened.

Following his gaze, I saw how quickly the day was winding down. In the increasingly dim light of his shop, the shadows grew deep. To our unquiet minds, in any one of them might lurk a monster.

He turned back to me and went on, his voice pitched somewhat lower than before. "Somehow this false thing has clawed it's way back across the boundaries — or, rather, God has allowed it to do so."

This was uncharacteristic of him, to stray into faith, and it unsettled me. "But why? What purpose could there be?"

Burke offered me the rueful smile of a skeptic. "Who's to say? You've often told me that Terminus sets things to His purpose and that nothing falls outside the boundary of His lines."

Knowing him too well, I did not bristle at his gentle teasing. Burke's faith ran deeper than that thin, cynical facade. He believed on some level, I knew, even if he did not entirely accept it of himself.

"Who's to say?" he asked, serious once more. "But if He has opened the door to this abomination, it is apparent that you play a role in His purpose. If you truly believe in your God..."

"...and I do..."

"...then it seems obvious to me that it falls to you to exorcise this monster, to drive out this corruption." He rubbed one hand against the other, clapping them together for warmth. "You have to restore the boundaries that have been trespassed between life and death."

"But surely . . . a *monster?* Who's to say that this isn't just some crazed villager or, worse yet, a contingent of concerned citizens intent on sending a message?" It seemed to me more

70

likely to me that some human agent, however cruel or crazed, was responsible for the events. I wasn't inclined to accept this theoretical monster of his.

Burke dismissed my rational approach with a scornful twist of his mouth, adding more to my growing armful of books. "The signs are too clear."

"Signs?"

"The hallmarks of folklore: The drained corpses, the desecrations in the graveyard, the strange sounds in the fields..." he shrugged.

"Those could be the work of anyone trying to scare me."

His eyes met mine, steady and unblinking. "Only the rarest of books tell of these things, most of them banned. Name me one person in our pleasant little hamlet that has the knowledge to impersonate such a mythology."

"Apart from the two of us, you mean?"

"And you didn't know until I told you," he said smugly.

"So you're the culprit," I grinned at him. "I should have known."

Burke's face grew serious. "Don't even joke of such things. One aspect all of the stories agree on is that a blight like this can overtake entire communities, corrupting even the purest of hearts. In such cases, only fire and death can finally free the afflicted from their torment."

"That sounds rather aggressive."

Burke nodded. "To put it mildly, yes. But remember that you battle not against flesh and blood — at least, not anymore."

He stopped for a moment to look at me. "Hazard has set loose her children in this land once again," he said at last, somber and thoughtful. His words sent a chill through me. The invocation of Hazard was as uncommon then as it is today. And from an agnostic such a Burke, even more disturbing. Few things could move him to such conviction.

Hazard and her children, prowling the darkness on the outskirts. A horrible thought.

Though contemporary minds in these times view her as no more than a fairy tale ghoul, back then we believed in Hazard and kept well inside the boundaries set by Terminus. Many of us had heard the stories, passed down from our forebears. In those times we knew how closely the borders were prowled, how easily and how often trespass might occur.

But even so, a monster?

"This thing has been given the strength to claw back into life once more. It has strength enough for that, it has strength enough to defeat you."

He was right. I am not, by inclination as well as vocation, a man of confrontation. Nor am I conversant with the vocabulary of battle, and courage is not part of my character. The hardest struggle I face each day is keeping up with the inevitable and exigent ebb of life in my village. My profession offered me no experience to match my strength against that of the unwilling dead.

"So what can I do, then? God would not give me this task if I were doomed to fail at it."

"Are you so sure about that?" Burke asked, stooping to read the faded gilt bindings on a shelf in front of him. "Plenty have done precisely that. Did the fault lie with them or with their God?"

"'Terminus does not raise us up in order to watch us fall,'" I quoted.

"Maybe so." He rose with a grunt, tossing another tome on top of my ever-growing stack. "That's your strength, then. That's your weapon."

"What is?" I shifted my grip to keep the books from sliding out of my arms under this new weight.

"Your faith," he said, heading up the aisle.

I followed, ever the apprentice. "No weapons or wiles will serve you so well as that." He led me back through the shelves to the desk at the back of the store.

I set the books down on the desk, massaging my sore hands. "Are there no weapons then?" I asked.

"Oh no, we have weapons." Burke said, gesturing to the stack of books. "We just have to discover what they are."

We pored over his books together late into the night, drawing out every anecdote, however obscure, to lend depth to our understanding of the battle to come. And for every point of agreement we uncovered, a hundred more contradictions shouted down my confidence. But Burke was right, in the end. We did find one or two charms that I hoped might prove useful in the days to come.

Finally, just before dawn, Burke put his head in his hands.

"You'll have to go to her," he told me.

"Who?" I did not look up from the arcane text opened in front of me — though, truth be told, I'd been reading the same page for nearly an hour.

"The Eastern woman, the authoress." He raised his head. "To Cires Ling. Though it's nothing but a ghoulish fantasy, there may be some clue in her book that might help arm you against this abomination. Whatever she knows, whatever she may be able to pass on, it could prove useful to you."

"But what do I say to her?"

"Say to her..." he considered for a moment. "Say to her that her monster, or one of it's kindred, might be here among us."

"But what do I tell her? What is this thing?"

"Vampire." Burke told me quietly. "It is called a vampire."

In silence, we bent back over the books before us, waiting for dawn to come.

Chapter Fourteen

"Women do not weep, but for men and children."

— Lady Diana Ulster, *Proverbs from The Midlands*

The hollow fruit on the gate rattled as I entered Cires Ling's garden for the last time.

Within, I found every plant, shrub, and leaf had withered, the lush growth crumbling under the touch of some unknown blight. Nothing had been spared.

But whatever had struck this place, it was neither natural not happenstance. Even the stones that marked out the gently curving paths had been scattered, their boundaries deliberately blurred beyond recognition.

The head of the stone demon lay on the blackened lawn among other shattered fragments, the baleful gaze accusing me as I passed through the bare skeletal trees clutching at the flat cast of the sky.

The house squatted over the ruins, windows staring blankly down upon the tragedy.

Whoever had done this, they'd been comprehensive in their vandalism. My head swam at the sheer scope of the destruction. I could not imagine the force of will and effort it took to dismantle the former beauty of the place. It seemed beyond even the petty hate and prejudice of the villagers.

I wandered in this new wasteland, fearful of what grisly discoveries I might have to confront should I venture up to the house.

I found her sitting by the pond where the elegant, iridescent fish once swam — their tarnished carcasses drifting lazily on the greasy surface of the water, gutted and ruined forever.

She did not look up at my approach, nor ask my purpose. With the sleek, sad beauty of her face unveiled, I realized she was not past the birthing age. For a moment I hesitated, uncertain in my transgression and fearful of rebuke.

Seemingly oblivious to my trespass, she spoke — her voice so low and measured that I had to move closer in order to hear.

"You want to know about monsters."

So she knew, then. I nodded. It never occurred to me to ask how she had anticipated my purpose.

It was a long time before she spoke again...

"I have heard a story told — not in my lands, but another — and it is the story of the first people.

"Now, the God of that time — and I do not know which God it was — shaped the first people from the earth, the mud, the dust.

"In that time, the God of that place had made man and woman as one, male and female together, joined here..." she placed a delicate hand behind her, at the base of her spine.

"A garden was given to them and responsibility to find the names of the things they saw there. So the man and woman spent their days going about their work, speaking to each other over their shoulder, always together.

"Soon, they fell in love as was natural and good and what the God of that time had intended.

"But their lips could not reach and neither could they love one another as they desired. So when the God of that place came next to visit, they prayed for Him to draw a line between them and allow them their freedom to do what they desired.

"The God of that time took mercy on them and did as they asked.

"For the first time they each saw the face and form of their beloved. Their love feasted upon the sight and grew stronger than before. So consumed, they did not think to thank the God of that place, nor did they notice when He departed.

"They joined then, together once more, this time face to face. And it was good."

A chill wind rattled through the stripped branches overhead. Cires Ling waited as the bony fingers of the willow stirred the surface of the pond. Once it had passed, she continued.

"And, after a time, they spent their love and returned to their work together in the garden. But no longer did they have to scuttle like crabs back to back, and so their work was sooner and better accomplished than before. And yet, it took them much longer to complete, for each was so distracted by the other and stopped often to join together again in the way of men and women."

I confess I blushed at this. Yet Cires Ling took no notice.

"A day came when the God of this time returned once more to walk in the garden and take joy in what He had made. He called for the man to come and walk with Him and tell Him the names of things. But the man did not answer.

"So the God went looking for His man in the garden. And it was in His garden that He found him.

"There they were — joined together, face to face.

"The God of that time spoke to His man: COME AND WALK WITH ME.

"But His man, busy with his woman, did not hear nor answer.

"And the God of that time said: I MADE YOU BOTH, ONE AND TOGETHER. YET YOU BEGGED OF ME TO SEPARATE WHAT I HAD MADE, ONE FROM THE OTHER. WHY NOW DO I FIND YOU JOINED AGAIN? WHY DO YOU NOT COME TO ME WHEN I CALL? WHY DO YOU NOT HEARKEN WHEN I SPEAK? I AM GOD AND I AM ANGRY.

"Then the God of that time separated them once more. And His man was very angry, saying to Him: *You gave her to me.*

"The God answered: I GIVE AND I TAKE. I AM GOD. WHO ARE YOU?

"And His man answered: *I am Man and she is mine, not yours.*

"So the God of that time drove woman out of the garden and into the shadow, all for the pride of His man.

"Once woman had gone, He asked again: WHO ARE YOU?

"And His man answered: *I am alone.*

"The God of that time said: COME AND WALK WITH ME.

"But His man replied: *I am Man. I will not walk with God. I walk alone.*

"As he has ever since."

She sighed then, this beautiful woman. I could not tell if it was an affectation of her performance or if she truly felt it.

"Now woman, with the help of man, had made something of her own and she carried it away with her out of the garden. After a time, she brought it forth in shadow and when it had reached its age, it faced its mother and together in the darkness they made more in kind company to fill the shadow.

"In time, there were many of them and in the shadow their mother smiled . . . while somewhere else, in what used to be a garden, Man walked alone and apart from the God of that time.

"As he is walking still."

The evening rested heavily upon us both.

I did not speak.

She looked up at me, her face as smooth and pale as an egg. "That is the story I've been told."

Having little or no experience with authors, I asked "It is one of your own?"

To my instant regret, her brow wrinkled. "I have no stories of my own. They are all given by the gods."

"But you wrote it?"

She frowned, doubling my anxiety. "I am not a god. I did not, I cannot create these things. They are given to me and so I give them to you."

"But you're a writer," I protested. "I've heard of your fame. I saw the books you left for me."

She faced me and, with the last light of the day on her face, I saw at last the woman for whom poor Gaines had given up his life. And I understood.

"My books, my fame..." she did not quite sigh. "They are nothing. None but gods shape the chaos, none but gods can raise something out of the shadow."

I did not dare to say I did not understand. I did not have to.

She sighed again, saying "You came, wanting to know of monsters. I have told you of monsters . . . now go your way with this knowledge."

I stood there a few moments longer, waiting for something more. Yet she did not speak to me again.

I left through that cursed, rattling gate — left her alone, turned my back on that damned, beautiful face and left her to stare into the stagnant waters of her pool.

I have not seen her again in this life.

CHAPTER FIFTEEN

"Ashcroft resolved himself that he would speak with her father.
The time had come to make his feelings known and speak plainly,
regardless of the consequence. Though the patriarch had long since
harboured an obvious dislike for him, he had no doubt that a formal
presentment of his intentions would be, in time, accepted on its own
merits. He was, of course, quickly proven wrong."

— Emily Shackley, *The Unsuitable Suitor*

Through the fields I went, beneath an evening stretched full
across the sky like a blindfold.

But I did not go alone.

I was aware that someone was following me. And I — who had
worked with scores of the dead, who had "entertained familiars by
firelight" — I was afraid. For, whoever it was, they were not only
following . . . with every step, they came closer, approaching fast on
my heels. I quickened my pace a measure and I heard theirs increase
as well, whispering through the tall grasses like the wind.

When I could stand it no further, I stopped and turned to face the
shadow waiting nearby. The evening light gone dim, no more could I
see of them than a dark smudge against the sky.

I heard the figure draw breath, prepare to speak, and then stop.

I waited.

I thought of running. I thought to pray.

I thought of my sister and of the woman on the balcony.

Like anyone who hears Death's tread on the landing, I was
reminded of unfinished business.

Moreover, I had not yet taken an apprentice. I did not know who would bury my body when this thing slaughtered me out here on the lonely road.

Save for my sister, I might not even be mourned.

Then there spoke a voice so young and sweet that I nearly laughed with relief: "You do not know me, sir, but I am acquainted with your sister."

This was not the voice of a monster but of someone known to me. It was the voice I had heard the night before, serenading my sister. It was the voice of her lover.

"Indeed?" I could not help but note the hesitation in his voice, the social awkwardness of the young. I admit I felt something like sympathy towards him already, though we had just met — and no small amount of envy either. I would never know the frankness of love expressed and returned.

"I found her of late, walking in the fields by night. I should say, rather, that we found each other. And, I must confess, we are each the other's now."

I may have smiled at this, I might have been shocked. I do not recall. "Indeed?"

He must have perceived some disapproval in my tone, for he rushed to respond. "Please, I must apologize for this boldness of mine. I assure you of my integrity and devotion. You can be certain that she returns my admirations in kind."

"I have no doubt of this," I replied. "I know something of your romance already."

"Then she has told you of me, of my affections?"

I smiled at this and shook my head. "No, indeed . . . but I do not sleep so soundly."

"I'm sorry, I do not understand."

"Whispered conversations in the night never sound so quiet as lovers think. Neither so their songs nor their dances. And the nighttime hours only make them louder."

I chuckled. "I have, I must myself confess, eavesdropped on your mutual admirations. And I know my sister's voice. I have no doubt that she loves you."

Squinting into the gloom, I said "But these darker hours do nothing for my eyes. Come, let me meet you properly at last."

He wavered a moment, a mere shadow against the darkening sky. I could see his outline blotting out those few, early stars, but nothing more.

I stepped forward and raised my hand to accept his, but he moved back from me deeper into the safety of the shadows.

"My dear fellow," I said to the youth. "I assure you that I am not opposed to your intentions. You needn't fear me, of all people."

But he did not relent or return.

You must be very young indeed, I thought to myself.

He said "I apologize for my behavior, sir. I confess that I am of low status and somewhat ashamed of my position in this life."

"Tosh," I waved his concerns away. "These things matter not to me, nor to my sister."

"Yes. Yes, she is the jewel of your bloodline."

It was a strange expression and, like much of his phraseology, it rang odd to my ear. "I am curious, son . . . how is it that you knew me?"

"I'm afraid I don't quite follow your question," the shadow replied

"How is it that you knew me to belong to my sister? Have we made some acquaintance prior to this?"

I was intrigued by this fellow — his youth, his easy familiarity with me and my office. I tried to place him among those I knew in the village, unsuccessfully.

"I saw her face in yours," he replied.

I had not cause for surprise, but his remark took me aback. As I had not seen my sister in many years, I'd forgotten our resemblance. While my face in the mirror each morning had grown old, hers in my memory had not. She remained in some way, in all ways, the child that I had only last seen when I began my training.

But, of course, she was a child no longer.

"I see. Well, she will be waiting for me — for us both, I expect. Come and go with me."

I began walking again towards home, glancing from time to time in order to confirm that the boy in the shadows was still with me. I could not see his face. It was too dark for that.

We were, each of us, quiet for some time. But it was I who broke the silence: "Are you from the village, then? Or do you come from one of the hillside families?" I wasn't sure which I preferred. I hoped that, whoever his people were, I would find them tolerable as relatives.

There came no reply from the shadow against the stars.

"Apart from yesternight," I remarked, I hoped, casually. "I do not believe I know your voice."

My companion was a moment or two in coming to an answer. "Yes, there's no reason you should know it or me. We might have had some small contact in the past but it was nothing more than brief, and not such that I think you would recall."

"Perhaps you could remind me while you stop at our manor. I expect my sister will be rising soon. She will, I'm sure, be delighted to see you."

To my surprise, he declined. "I had intended to visit Miranda sometime later this evening, sir. And although your invitation is most welcome, I must beg your gracious release. I have other matters to attend to. I do not wish to impose but, if you are so inclined to extend your invitation, perhaps I might visit you another time."

"You are welcome in our house," I answered.

In the dark, I heard him smile. I am sure of it, even now.

"I am grateful. It is most appreciated."

Then he was gone. I saw his form receding against the horizon. The distance made him look very young indeed, nearly a child.

Then, turning my own way, I walked on towards my home — no longer thinking on monsters and desecrations, but rather of the sound of my sister's laughter in the night.

A happy thought. I might have smiled myself. I might have wept. I do not recall.

Chapter Sixteen

"When the time comes, every undertaker is called to face a loss of their own — be it a friend or family member, be it to mortality or matrimony. In any case, the lessons learned early in your apprenticeship will help you stay true to your vocation. This release is the undertaker's professional responsibility and it supersedes whatever other concerns might distract you from your duty to, quite simply, accept the fact that you need to let go of the life that's already escaped."

— Oliver Gast, *Notes from a Life Among the Dead*

Brother,

I have met a man.

I do not know what you may think of this. I do not know if you approve. But I do know that my heart is his. He has rescued me from the loneliness of this life with the greatest gift imaginable. I hope you may one day know such gifts for yourself.

I do not know what our plans will be, nor where they will lead us. He is somewhat young in this world and everything is to him still new and wonderful. As he has shown me wonder, so too will I show him.

Brother, he is my life and my soul.

We have been apart so long, you and I.

I know you will not deny me this joy, and I thank you for your love.

The dumbwaiter gaped open before me — that dark well at the bottom of which I lived — straining to hear my sister's faint voice from above.

I closed it and, still holding her note, went out onto the balcony at the back of the house.

Above, the sky was clear and dry. No mist hid the stars from me this night.

Below, the gravestones and monuments were pale against the darkness. A yellow square of light fell across the graveyard, cast by my sister's open window above.

Waiting for her lover to return, of course.

I had no plans to take a wife in my time. I hadn't the patience to undergo the endlessly formal rituals of selection and courtship. Those carefully choreographed couplings, the lonely and distant obligation, the tug of separation across an impassible boundary had no appeal for me.

Yet there was no reason my sister should not be happy. Once I might have expected her to offer herself back to the profession, a suitable helpmeet for one of my caste. Certainly her own life of solitude had prepared her for the role and she might have, in time, found a man and a place where contentment would make do for happiness.

But no longer.

I knew, of course, that she would leave with him. I would take full possession of the house and continue on in my service until my own years came to their lonely end.

I reread her note by the light of the stars, noting that she had not signed it. I wondered if it was an oversight on her part, or perhaps a familiarity between us. It's possible, I suppose, that time and neglect had taken her name from her.

My thoughts were interrupted by a sound from below, a voice rising from the graveyard. I saw a dark form moving among the pale stones. My first thought was of the monster, that it had returned.

Then the figure split apart and ran through the plots — laughing, doubled, like twin beads of mercury across a dark mirror.

My sister and her lover.

I watched them embrace and spin together amongst the graves, much as I had eavesdropped on their dancing the night before.

My twin laughed, joyful and wild. She threw her arms out in abandon, turning as she raised her face — far more pale than the gravestones — to the stars.

Her lover answered her with laughter of his own, and with his song so familiar and yet foreign to my ears.

And then I was on the path, running down to meet them with no clear thought in my head.

CHAPTER SEVENTEEN

"Suspicions, amongst thoughts, are like bats amongst birds, they ever fly by twilight."

— Sir Francis Bacon, from *Of Suspicion*

Though my eyes were blind with fear, my frantic feet fell sure on the familiar, well-worn path.

I thought of my sister's voice from the night before, a whisper floating down from her window.

A whisper, an invocation. A call to love from love.

I thought of her hand, writing the words: *Brother, he is my life and my soul.*

And Burke, his voice low and cautious as he recited the names of monsters: *Nosferatu, Wampyr, Drakul...*

Before the dumbwaiter, my sister's note clutched in my hand: *I have met a man.*

Hampton and the others in the village, chafing over a boy with bad blood, buried in their holy dirt: *Why would someone bury a child so far from their own land?*

A family cursed with bad blood.

I heard the fruit rattling on the gate, pecked dry by the birds. I saw withered flowers at every grave and Cires Ling sitting in her ruined garden, telling me of the birth of monsters.

The boy's uncle, his voice gnawing at the edges of my mind: *Open the grave, release whatever evil might be resting there.*

A bowl of eggs, the weasel at work.

The uncle's voice, like scraps of paper clinging to my memory: *The ninth regret approaches.*

Burke's earnestness: *These stories, they may be true.*

Poor Mason, pale and drained on the slab.

The poor boy's desecrated grave.

The shadow that followed me through the fields.

That song, calling my sister's name.

The lonely bird, ringing across the night.

His voice: *I had intended to visit Miranda sometime later this evening, sir.*

How pale my twin looked, dancing with a monster amongst the graves.

Nosferatu. Wampyr. Drakul.

And as I ran, I prayed.

CHAPTER EIGHTEEN

"I can heal these father's wounds:
your family has fed no grave,
all your people are alive."

— Seamus Heaney, *Sweeney Astray*

I faced the two of them there in the graveyard.

My sister was in his arms and, at my approach, she turned her face towards me.

I recognized nothing in her eyes — those eyes I had not seen but in dreams for so many years — nothing familiar remained, only dead madness.

I threw myself at them, driving them apart.

Her insane eyes met my own. Her face contorted, drooling rage. Her skin, very pale. Her throat torn across one side. There was little blood and the flesh looked very cold.

Nothing familiar remained.

"Sister, flee this place. You have been ensnared by a monster and a monster you have become."

She made as if she might lunge for me, but I held her at bay with the strength of my voice and my love.

"Sister, forsake this creature. There is nothing but death for you here."

She fell to her knees and wept hotly, but either in rage or sorrow I could not know.

She looked up, those ruined eyes scraping across mine, her voice rising from that savaged throat.

"But I love him..." she whispered.

My tears matched her own. "Sister, there is nothing in him but death. Give him over, give him back to the shadow."

She howled, throwing her head back and exposing that torn throat, lifting that tormented second maw to gape in protest to the stars.

She rose, hands clawing at the air between us. And again came a whisper from that dreadful double mouth: "Then . . . I stay . . . daughter and sister . . . of death. I stay . . . lover and bride . . . of death as well. Death shall . . . be denied me . . . no longer."

I could not help but scream at her: "In the name of our family, of our father and the blood we share between us, leave this place."

She stared, insane and uncomprehending.

"In the name of God, Miranda, go!"

I flung my words at her and she, wilting from them, fled back into the shadows and towards the manor.

He was young, the monster I turned to face after she had gone, young and very small. And full of life, far more so than when his mother and uncle had brought him to me for burial.

He'd remained silent up until now, but he smiled at me as my sister fled. His lips, smeared with blood — my sister's blood — were very dark against his pale skin.

He laughed, driving me backward with the sheer force of his voice. And then I knew full well that true evil was here before me.

His voice, so rich and deep, spanning lifetimes. Yet from the mouth of a youth barely in his teens? It was an abomination, a profane and vile thing, a disgusting mockery of Terminus and His dominion.

The boy, the monster, moved in. "I am not of your land nor of your blood, undertaker. Your weak words have no authority over me."

I staggered backwards as if that obscene voice pushed against me.

The creature laughed, his voice driving me back further until I fell against a nearby gravestone.

"Know the name of what you fear. I am the monster, the demon and the dragon. A child of Lilith and a son of Hell. Your petty line-walking God has bound me in this flesh for all eternity, damned me beyond the reach of life or death."

Cold hands against my throat, a child's hands, lifted my face to his. "Look upon me, cousin. Watch me feed."

His head swayed with a serpent's syncopation, his eyes hooked deep into mine — wicked, aged things . . . dark jewels set in a rotting mask of flesh. The rank air spilled out of his open mouth, all dirt and rot.

"God," I managed to gasp, "Deliver your faithful servant from this unholy thing."

The creature blanched and shrank back at the invocation of the holy, his eyes rolling in fear and clutching his head.

I felt a glimmer of hope and tried to rise.

Chuckling, the monster grinned. I realized in despair: It had been mocking me.

"Your god is not here, brother-in-law. You are alone."

Rising up over me like a wave, the monster threw me back against the gravestone once more. I stuck my temple as I fell. The world stuttered in and out of blackness. Through the storm, those terrible eyes swept across mine once more.

I clawed at the stone, my hands seizing upon a mourning wreath hanging there. Galvanized with panic, I crushed the pale flowers in my fists. A pungent, faintly warm scent rose up and I felt some of my strength return.

Moly flowers, unwilted.

Sorcerer's garlic, Burke had told me, *one of the few weapons we have against the shadowkind.*

The monster faltered, his face twisting in revulsion as the scent spread towards him.

Pink bile spilled from that awful gape, splattering across my hands and arms as I thrust the pungent buds forward to drive the creature back. No pantomime mock of victory now, his howl of rage and pain was genuine as I pressed him on backwards through the graveyard. Though he tried to hold his ground once or twice, ever snarling, the moly overpowered him and he retreated once more.

Soon he realized our destination, discovering that I'd been driving him back towards his own grave. The monster laughed, saying "You think you can cage me once more? That petty weed will wither soon enough."

"There's more than flowers," I told him.

He grinned. "Do your worst. Bury me again and go home to sit and wait for me to come and drain your life."

Strengthened by the scent and by my God, I replied through clenched teeth. "You shall never drink of my blood, monster."

His smile grew sharper. "Oh no, not I . . . no, your own sister shall feed on you, brother-in-law. She will draw your soul into the shadow, not I. She is mine now. Mine for good. I have drunk of her and she of me."

He spat at me, laughing. "And no pretty flower can bring her back."

I did not falter but I must confess I felt fear at his words. I was so ignorant of his kind and their ways. But it was no matter. I had to fulfill the task that God had given me, regardless of the outcome. Perhaps, once it was all over, Burke could offer some guidance on how I could help cure my sister of this affliction.

Had I but known.

I pressed forward. Behind him, the monster's grave loomed dark against the night, the ground gaping open.

The creature howled at me one last time before it spun and fled, diving straight into the open grave waiting for it.

I heard a gruesome scraping from the pit and, approaching cautiously, I peeked over the edge in time to see the lid of the coffin clamp into place.

I could hear him in there, laughing back up at me in triumph. Yet I could not help but smile with some small victory of my own. The monster thought I could not bottle him for long, but he'd not counted on Burke's diligent instruction.

Breaking the wreath in my hands, I laid the flowers — their odor still quite strong — around the rim of the grave before I retreated to Mason's shack. Inside, I cleaned my face and hands of the monster's vile stink, rinsing away that horrid bile.

Facing the mirror, I stared thoughtfully into my own eyes for a long moment. Then, drawing back my fist, I shattered my reflection.

Filling my pockets with the broken shards, I took up a shovel and left the shack. When I returned to the grave, the flowers remained undisturbed. The monster was contained.

I dug at the edges with my shovel, widening the grave. It was long, difficult work and I paused often to rest, my hands and shoulders singing with the effort of it. Soon the hole had spread out into a smooth, round hollow in the earth. It was a grave no longer but a humble cup in which I hoped to catch the dawn.

My labor finished, I threw the shovel aside and sat down with my back against the casket to wait. The scent of moly spread over me, warm and peaceful. I looked up at the manor, dark against the stars. I wondered for the first time if the dead resented the presence of the house looming over them or if it was a comfort? Perhaps they did not care at all.

One window — my sister's — shone brightly, like a lighthouse in the darkening storm. I thought of her there, pacing the floors, mourning her lover. I tried to contain thoughts, to capture words that I could say to her once the dawn had come and my duties here were finished.

God is kind; He forgives those children who stray outside the boundaries. Of that I had no doubt. And my sister was no rebel, I knew. Perhaps with Burke's help, I could in time find a remedy for her affliction — romantic and spiritual — and draw her back from where she had stayed too close to the borderlands of life.

She might never forgive me, I knew. But I could try.

The chill fingers of night pressed into my bones, tugging me away into a shallow sleep. And when it waned, I watched her window while I waited for the dawn to come.

Once I've scraped this abomination from the earth, I told myself, *I will help her however I can.*

She might never forgive me, but she would be safe.

Of that I had no doubt.

Chapter Nineteen

"Après tout le deuil, on rêve."

— from the unpublished journals of Michel-Robert Gaines

I dreamt I was an actor on the stage.

I dreamt I was dead.

I dreamt of pen and ink, of words flowing across the page and of the dark blood of books.

I dreamt of withered fruit strung from the rafters of my library, rattling faintly in the breeze.

These dreams and more came to me that night, my mind a shattered mirror seething with visions.

I dreamt of my house, the roof caved in, and of a solitary pale figure that traced wandering paths in hollow footsteps across the warped and dusty floors.

These dreams and more did I see.

This and more was shown to me, before I woke.

CHAPTER TWENTY

"None of the rites matter. The dead go their way whether we pray or no."

— Walter Martin Lincoln, *Lazarus: The Reluctant Resurrection*

The morning sun rose like a forgotten friend, suddenly remembered and welcome.

I stretched out to let those thin, early rays reach my stiff, complaining muscles. It would be some time before I was warm.

No matter, I had time to wait while the light played across the carved lid of the casket. I imagined the air inside growing warmer by the second as it soaked up the heat of dawn. I thought of my sister's monstrous lover within, twisting against the hot, unseen hand that reached in to stifle him.

It was a small cruelty and I am not ashamed to say that I savored it, as welcome as the sunlight after my long watches in the chill night.

From a nearby grave, I took up another wreath of moly and crushed the aromatic blossoms and leaves against the lid of the coffin, staining it with their dark juice.

Turning out my pockets, I scattered the bright shards of Mason's mirror in a wide circle around the casket and over it, the broken fragments catching the early light of the sun.

It was beautiful, I had to admit — no matter what manner of creature crouched, suffered, within.

The sun cleared the hills, stretching its long fingers across the fields, fanning life and warmth into this dead, grey land.

I took up my shovel and raised it over the coffin, waiting for the dawn to reach me.

A prayer on my lips, I brought down the shovel and shattered the lid of the casket and stood back to watch what followed.

Sunlight, Burke had told me.

And under that light, a flower of rage and pain blossomed out of the open casket.

I smiled, grim and savoring the destruction.

From out of the grave rose a dark and vicious mass to burst against the sky. Twisting shadows of scorched meat and bone flailed, skewered on the morning rays of the sun. The shards of mirror I'd scattered around the coffin caught the dawn and threw it back in the face of the horrible mass, carving the life away from this poor, doomed foundling of Hazard.

A great, agonized howl rang out . . . the voice of evil echoing through the eternity it had been denied.

A satisfying sight, watching it tumble back into the casket all blackened and splintered beyond repair. A feeble hiss rose up from the mess, and the bones rattled for a while before, finally, falling silent.

"Requiescat en pace." And I would have pronounced more — and more damning — litanies over the ruin, but my voice failed me at the end.

For, in the casket — staring back up at me with hollow sockets — not one, but two greasy, blackened skulls grinned at me.

Two skulls.

And, as I am trained in the artful language of bones, in a glance I knew that one was male and the other female.

Two skeletons, mingled in the ashes.

Male and female, unmade by my hand.

I turned away, looking back up to the manor looming over the graveyard, to the window that stood open to the sun. I knew then that single, staring eye was blind and had been so all night.

No, my sister did not wait above. But, rather, she lay here before me now, intertwined in the arms of her lover.

Abandoned to Hazard and damnation.

Lost to me. Forever.

Chapter Twenty-One

"And every woe a tear can claim,
Except an erring sister's shame."

— George Gordon Noel, from *The Giaour*

I scattered their bones across the hollow place I'd made around the grave, intermingling the scorched ivory with the shards of mirror and wilted garlic blossoms.

I shattered their skulls, brutal as it may seem. I do not know what I felt, frustration or necessity. I cannot say now.

And then I went home.

I do not know how long it was before I dared venture into the upper halls and rooms so long closed to me. But when I did, they revealed to me all the secrets of my sister's life which I had never even guessed. She too, apparently, had her own passion for books. I found one room stacked nearly to the rafters with them. Most of them were romances in the popular, common vein.

"Pastes," Burke would have called them, sneering even as he sold them to her. He might have told me. I might have guessed. It might have made a difference.

She must have been so lonely.

I could not help but retreat from this pathetic discovery. With nowhere to go, I wandered the manor until I finally came to rest in my own library once more.

As the gloaming filled my windows, I took up one of the books Burke had given me, one of Cires Ling's banned, beautiful novels.

So gentle, I turned those thin paper pages. The strange, foreign characters flitting under my fingers like a flight of birds scattered across a winter sky.

The slender volume fell open to an illustration. An elegant representation of a dragon-faced infant suckling at his mother's breast — the child's thin hand twisted in her hair, her head pulled back and throat taut, mouth gaping in horror.

Very lifelike. Familiar.

I might have guessed.

That evening, on flames of moly, I laid the pages of Cires Ling's rarest masterpiece, watching them blacken and burn one by one. Once they had cooled, I crushed the fragile gray embers between my fingers and I wept.

That night I dreamt I was wandering through the village, ruined and abandoned. Every home stood open, every life within nothing more than a hollow husk drained by the monster's appetites. Men and women, all the children . . . none had been spared.

Alone, I tended to them and, all alone, I laid them to rest.

I felt nothing. It was no matter, no great concern.

I was going to perform this duty for them all, sooner or later.

My long labor complete, I retired to my manor and waited, wondering what would come first: The dawn or the first faint stirrings down in the graveyard below?

Since then, since that night, I have not dreamed. In these long years past, now I take to my bed only when I cannot stand the silence any longer and I wait. Eventually sleep comes for me and I let myself drift, grateful, across a still pool of dreamless, shallow water.

CHAPTER TWENTY-TWO

"Hoc sustinete, majus ne veniat malum."

— Phaedrus, *Fables*

The house of Cires Ling stood long rotting in the fields. Inside, the tapestries gathered dust while porcelain faces faded and crumbled beneath the slow, insistent fingertips of time. Only a blackened patch of earth remains where once her garden thrived.

Eventually, even the house fell.

In the village, the people nod their heads and whisper pious judgments on me even as they rely on my services. Long years have passed and the dark gossip has made me a celebrity of sorts. They fear me now more than ever.

Among them, only Burke knows how close to the gates the children of Hazard once prowled and only he knows who spared them. Yet he keeps his peace and continues to buy their lives from them while I dispose of the remnants.

A thinning harvest for us both, year to year.

And if the great God Terminus still walks the boundaries, I cannot say. Within, in our ignorance, we do His work as best we can whether He does or not.

The manor is mine now, whole and complete and alone. Only my footfalls echo there as I wander in the night.

Outside, no strange cries ring out across the fields.

Flowers no longer wither prematurely in the graveyard below.

ACKNOWLEDGEMENTS

This book began as a dream back in 1993: I was alone, walking at dusk through the tall grass. Something followed close behind, something monstrous and insane with its own evil.

That was all I remembered when I woke.

I spent a lot of time alone in those days. But I'm fortunate to have found more than a few friends since then.

My old friend Jeff Mauerman had the dubious honor of being the first to read this story, back when my dreams of being a writer far outshone my skill. And although that's still the case, it is the encouragement from friends like Maureen Abele and Gavin Ashley Hall that keep me dreaming and writing.

Regrettably, I do not have enough room here to name all of my online friends, followers, and fans — but I cannot thank you enough for all your enthusiasm and evangelism. Keep spreading the word, kids.

But most of all, this book would not exist without my wife Keeley's support and encouragement. Thanks to her, I no longer walk — or dream — alone.

T.M. Camp
October 9, 2009
Somewhere in the Midlands

About the Author

Despite having a grown up job for most of his adult life, T.M. Camp has still managed to find the time to author over thirty plays, many short stories and poems, and two novels. Needless to say, he doesn't sleep very much.

His plays have been produced by theatres in California, Michigan, Iowa, and Tennessee. His short fiction and poetry has appeared in various online journals and podcasts.

In 2008, he released his novels *Assam & Darjeeling* and *Matters of Mortology* as free audiobooks in 2008 through iTunes and on his website — where both are still available for free download.

In addition to a number of smaller, ongoing projects, T.M. is currently at work on his third novel, entitled *Pantheon*.

He lives in Grand Rapids, Michigan, with his excellent and lovely wife, as well as an indeterminate number of cats and children of variable age and intelligence.

For the first time in over a decade, the house he lives in is not haunted. And for some reason, this makes him a little sad.

www.ingramcontent.com/pod-product-compliance
Lightning Source LLC
Chambersburg PA
CBHW020619130626
46552CB00003B/1049